KNIGHT SIR LOUIS
AND THE
DRAGON
OF
DOOOOOOM!

www.guppybooks.co.uk

Praise for *Knight Sir Louis*

'I love these books so much! Mr Gum
levels of weird and brilliant!'
Jo Nadin

'What a hero! What a story! Sublime daftness on every page.'
Jeremy Strong

'Probably the funniest book I've ever
read. A masterclass in silliness!'
Gary Northfield, author of the *Julius Zebra* series

'Brimming with ludicrous magic and
fizzing with irresistible comedy.'
Peter Lord, co-founder of Aardman Animations

'The Brothers McLeod's scratchy penmanship and casual
attitude to the conventions of story-telling spin the fairy tale in
a new direction, as if Hans Christian Andersen had cornered
you in a pub and got his own yarn in the wrong order, or the
Brothers Grimm had squeezed up next to you with a Tupperware
box of home-made sandwiches on a long coach journey.'
Stewart Lee, comedian

'Will appeal to anyone who likes adventures and laughing.'
Philip Reeve

'One of the funniest, most original and random pieces
of children's literature you will read this year!'
My Book Corner

'Refreshing and entertaining . . . you will find yourself twisting
and turning the book as you laugh along at the puns and jokes.'
Books for Topics

KNIGHT SIR LOUIS

AND THE DRAGON OF DOOOOOOM!

by The Brothers McLeod

GUPPY
BOOKS

KNIGHT SIR LOUIS AND THE DRAGON OF DOOOOOOM!
is a GUPPY BOOK

First published in 2021 by
Guppy Books,
Bracken Hill,
Cotswold Road,
Oxford OX2 9JG

Text copyright © The Brothers McLeod

978 1 913101 42 8

1 3 5 7 9 10 8 6 4 2

The rights of The Brothers McLeod to be identified as
the author of this work has been asserted in accordance
with the Copyright, Designs and Patents Act 1988.

Papers used by Guppy Books are from well-managed
forests and other responsible sources.

GUPPY PUBLISHING LTD Reg. No. 11565833

A CIP catalogue record for this book is
available from the British Library.

Typeset in 13½/20 pt Adobe Garamond by
Falcon Oast Graphic Art Ltd, www.falcon.uk.com

Printed and bound in Great Britain by CPI Books Ltd

For Louis

SO WHO'S IN THIS

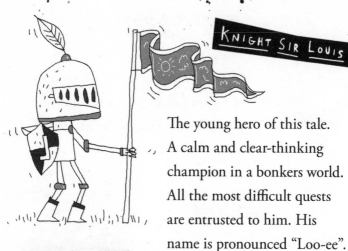

KNIGHT SIR LOUIS

The young hero of this tale. A calm and clear-thinking champion in a bonkers world. All the most difficult quests are entrusted to him. His name is pronounced "Loo-ee".

CLUNKALOT

The trusty mechanical steed. Sturdy, brave and always ready to join his beloved master Louis on a dangerous quest. Also loves flying and poetry.

BOOK EXACTLY?

MR CATALOGUE

This boar is a unique sort of piggywig. Loyal, willing to try anything once (or even twice), with a brain made "much more thinky" by magic.

PEARLIN

A young, self-taught wizard and inventor (or wizentor!). Always coming up with new and fun ways of using machines and magic.

KING BURT THE NOT BAD

The (mostly) kind and (usually) fair King of Squirrel Helm who lives in Castle Sideways.

DAVE THE SWORD

A magical sword recycled from a magic mirror. Likes reflecting magical spells, chopping up nasty things and singing. (Is an awful singer.)

QUEEN INCREDULOUS

The ruler of the Kingdom of Klaptrap. Believes toast is evil. Would like to be the ruler of the universe.

MERRY-JINGLES

An ambitious jester in the court of Queen Incredulous from a long line of hilarious fools.

KNIGHT SIR DAISY

Currently, champion knight for Queen Incredulous. At least, for now! Truth-seeker. Fact-lover. Doesn't believe toast is evil.

MYSTO

The greatest wizentor
ever known. Currently
missing! (Again.)

And last, but definitely not least . . .

BORAX

A fiendish double-headed dragon whose
only mission is to be really, really irritating
to as many people as possible.

CHAPTER 1

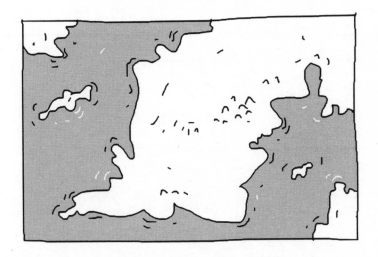

Oo yes. Let's start this book with a map. Come closer.

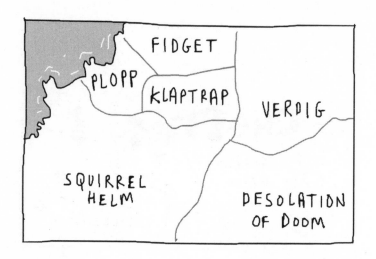

Closer.

No, not that close. Back up a bit.

2

Ah yes! It's a map of that famous, feared land . . .
the Desolation of Dooooom. Not to be confused
with Doo'oom which is a lovely little village by
the sea. They have a nice tea room with the best
cakes ever.

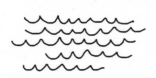

No, the Desolation of Doooooom doesn't have any tea rooms or cakes because it's a land inhabited by dragons. Doooooom Dragons are well known for being big, bad-tempered and for breathing blue fire. If a tea room did open in the Desolation of Doooooom, say at 8am in the morning, then it would be without a roof by 9am, the cakes set on fire by 10am, and all the bakers eaten by lunchtime.

Doooooom is not a pretty country. It's not the sort of place you'd find in a holiday brochure. Not unless you like taking your holidays inside a volcano. Most of it has been set on fire (several times) so that it's a dry, dusty place with hardly any trees or wildlife. The only other things that can survive there do so by living underground (like the burrowing three-humped camels).

So, you're probably thinking that these Doooooom dragons must be a terrible threat to their neighbours in the surrounding kingdoms?

Fortunately, most Dooooooom dragons are lazy and don't like long distance travel. They also try not to attract the attention of brave knights. Why? Because brave knights like daring adventures and turning dragon heads into wall ornaments.

So, usually the dragons just stay within the borders of Doooooom.

But . . .

. . . things have changed. Thanks to one dragon.

CHAPTER 2

Now, there are lots of different kinds of dragon in Dooooooom.

I'm not going to list them all. This isn't a biology textbook you know. All you need to know is that bi-dragons can be some of the most foul-tempered and they have two heads. A lot of the time the two heads don't like each other very much. This usually results in a very fiery argument and a very charred ex-dragon. But sometimes they get along. Those are the really dangerous ones. Like Borax.

This is Borax. I wouldn't get too close if I were you. This illustration is dangerous.

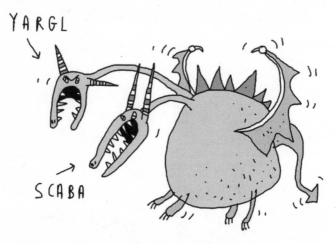

YARGL

SCABA

Borax's two heads have different names: Yargl Borax is on the left there. He's cruel, spiteful and CUNNING. Scaba Borax is on the right. She's quick-tempered, mean and CUNNING.

Borax started out life as an egg. They were just one of seven eggs. They were the smallest egg.

Even before Borax was born they could hear their dragon parents who would mock Borax's egg.

Stuff like that.

Maybe Yargl and Scaba could have turned out to be lovely and considerate if they'd been treated with kindness. We'll never know. Because even before they were born they were CUNNING. They put their heads together and came up with a plan. They decided to hatch out before the other eggs.

They waited until their parents had gone off to feed. Then they stretched and pushed and wriggled until they hatched themselves. Once they were out, they munched up all the other eggs. Then they dragged the nest over a big hole, stuck the egg shells back in the nest and waited for their parents to return.

When their parents came home and sat back on the nest . . . it fell into the hole taking their unfortunate parents with it. They were never seen again.

Yargl and Scaba never looked back.

Meanies.

HEY! THIS BOOK'S ABOUT KNIGHT SIR LOUIS ISN'T IT?

ALL I'VE HEARD ABOUT SO FAR IS A BUNCH OF DRAGONS.

PATIENCE! I'M SURE LOUIS WILL BE HERE VERY SOON.

BUT I DON'T WANT TO WAIT!

Okay. Fair enough. Let's quickly check in on Louis.

CHAPTER
BREAKFAST

As you can see, Louis is still getting ready for this book. Right now, he's cooking breakfast. Looks like eggs, beans and buttery crumpets with a glass of milk. Mmm.

CHAPTER 3

Now, let's head over to Castle Round-the-Twist in the kingdom of Klaptrap.

This very twisty castle is home to Queen Incredulous. Here are some of the things she believes:

TOAST IS EVIL!

OWLS ARE CATS with WINGS

34

IS THE Biggest NUMBER IN THE UNIVERSE

THE SEA ISN'T REALLY THERE

MOUNTAINS ARE MADE OF RUBBER

Queen Incredulous isn't the sort of queen to be distracted by things like facts or information. Once she's decided something is true, then nothing can change her mind. That's why she is very unhappy with her champion, Knight Sir Daisy.

Knight Sir Daisy is a brave, fearless knight. Since becoming the champion last year at the age of eleven, she hasn't really had the chance to fight dire dragons, or wayward wizards or ignoble knights.

She's been fighting for the truth! Here's a secret lecture she gave just last week to the Castle Round-the-Twist Union of Sciencey Thoughts and Ideas (or CRUSTI for short).

Hello everyone. Thanks for coming. Here's what I've discovered this week.

I went and had a look at the sea.

I know it's forbidden and the queen doesn't think it's there but . . .

. . . I decided to check it out.

Well. It turns out it IS there.

And it is both fun and dangerous depending on what you do with it.

I've also discovered . . .

Toast is hot bread.

Owls are birds.

Thirty-five is a bigger number than thirty-four.

Mountains are made of rocks.

At this point someone in the audience leapt up. It turned out to be Queen Incredulous herself in disguise. She was not happy.

I AM NOT HAPPY!

She had the whole society arrested and thrown onto the helter-skelter which slid down into her dungeon known as The Pits.

Before Knight Sir Daisy was

thrown down the slide, Queen Incredulous pointed at her and said, 'Ysiad ris thgink eeht bud I.'

Which is: 'I dub thee Knight Sir Daisy' but backwards. This was Queen Incredulous' way of unknighting her champion. Knight Sir Daisy was now just plain old Daisy. Daisy was sent down to join her CRUSTI chums in The Pits. Queen Incredulous dusted off her hands to show she was happy to be rid of them. Then she realised. 'Uh oh! Now I don't have a champion knight anymore.' So, she quickly promoted her jester 'Maxwell of Merry-Jingles' to the role.

KNIGHT SIR MERRY JINGLES

NOT VERY GOOD AT FIGHTING, JOUSTING OR BEING BRAVE. VERY GOOD AT AGREEING WITH QUEEN INCREDULOUS. LIKES READING. MOST RECENT BOOK:
'HOW TO BE EXTREMELY CUNNING' BY BARON SLY.

You'll be glad to hear this wasn't the end of Knight Sir Daisy. She had plans. But you'll have to wait to find out what they were.

CHAPTER 4

SURELY IT <u>MUST</u> BE TIME TO
INTRODUCE KNIGHT SIR LOUIS
TO THIS STORY ABOUT
KNIGHT SIR LOUIS?

You're quite right. We've waited far too long. Here he comes.

And there he goes. On Clunkalot, his robot horse, of course.

Come on. We'll have to run to keep up with him. While we are catching up, let's check in on a few details. Here's a handy Louis fact sheet.

FACTSHEET

NAME: LOUIS

RANK: KNIGHT, ALSO DEPUTY KING

WHERE: CASTLE SIDEWAYS, THE KINGDOM OF SQUIRREL HELM

BOSS: KING BURT THE NOT BAD

SKILLS: SWORD FIGHTING, PLANNING, AND MORE RECENTLY, PIANO (GRADE 1)

INTERESTS: BEING BRAVE

FAVOURITE COLOURS: STROBAFLUNGE (IT'S A KIND OF YELLOW)

FEARS: COMMON WASP, WOOD WASP, PAPER WASP, RED WASP, SINGING WASP, SHOUTING WASP, YODELLING WASP... BASICALLY WASPS.

CHAPTER 5

So, where is Louis going in such a hurry? Well, Borax has been flying out from the Desolation of Doooooom to have some nasty fun. Most recently Borax has paid a visit to the village of Much Kindling. Yargl and Scaba have just eaten four sheep, thirteen chickens and set fire to the village hall and half the houses.

The folks of Much Kindling had been preparing for an attack. Well . . . sort of. They had been hiding in the wettest place they knew, the local swimming pool. They'd been there for ages. They had been swimming up and down, up and down, and up and down some more. It was hard to tell who was wrinkly because they were old and who was wrinkly from all the time in the water.

On the plus side everyone was safe and feeling fitter than ever. Even better, all the children were now experts at front crawl and had earned their gold swimming proficiency badges.

Knight Sir Louis flew over the town on Clunkalot. The villagers were relieved to see him. They wondered, how was their hero going to save them? Maybe Clunkie was full of water. Maybe he was going to spit out a jet of ice-cold mist? But then Louis guided Clunkie up, higher and higher into the sky over the town.

'Why's he flying away?' said one villager.

'I bet he's got a plan!' said another.

He did have a plan. Once Louis was high enough, he reached inside Clunkie's inner compartment and pulled out a magical bazooka. It had been specially modified by Louis' friend Pearlin the Wizentor.

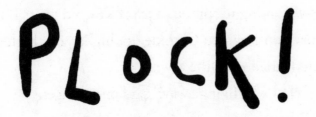

MAGICAL BAZOOKA
THAT ONCE BELONGED
TO AN EVIL WIZARD →

BAZOOKA FIXED UP TO
SHOOT OFF GOOD MAGICAL SPELLS

'Let's hope this works,' said Louis.
He fired!

PLOCK!

ZAP!
KABOOM!

The spell exploded in the sky above him. A moment later a little white cloud appeared. Another moment later it was ten times the size. Another moment and it was a thousand times the size! Then it turned into a dark purple rain cloud. Finally, the cloud reshaped into something resembling a giant tap. It turned itself on and it rained. A lot.

All the fires of Much Kindling were put out in a

moment. Almost immediately the tap turned itself off and disappeared. Blue skies returned and the sun got on with drying everything up. Clunkalot wrote a haiku poem to celebrate.

WHEN THE SKY CRIES TEARS,
THE FIRES OF EARTHLY ANGER
TURN TO STEAM'S EMBRACE.

Clunkie was very pleased with it. And so he should be. Later on, he entered it into the Seriously Smuglington Poetry Competition. The judges were so impressed it won First, Second and Third Prizes in the same year.

Unfortunately, the cloud spell split the magical bazooka in two. That was the last time Louis would be able to create a giant rain cloud to save the day.

Knight Sir Louis flew down on Clunkie and opened the doors to the swimming pool.

'It's all right,' he announced to the villagers. 'You can go back home now!'

'Thanks, but maybe later,' replied Lady Kindling, the leader of the town, 'we're in the middle of a water polo tournament right now.'

Knight Sir Louis thought about sticking around to cheer them on, but Clunkie received another alert. It was an email from the king, tagged urgent.

Return to Castle Sideways immediately by order

*of me, the king, King Burt the Not Bad! Pretty please
with a cherry on top. Bye-ee.*

Knight Sir Louis didn't need to be asked twice.
'Come on, Clunkie. Let's go!'

And now let us all come together and celebrate the birth of

CHAPTER FIVE AND A BIT

Isn't it a lovely chapter? It'll probably grow up to be a very big chapter one day. Something like Chapter Twenty-Nine. Hopefully it won't turn into a Chapter Thirty-Four. That would be unfortunate. Anyway, let's hope it becomes a chapter with something important to say. For now, though, it's just a little baby chapter. Coochee coochee coochee coo.

BURBLE BURBLE

CHAPTER 6

While Clunkie flew back to the castle, Knight Sir Louis decided to write a letter to his mother, the Champion Trixie. She was chief knight in the eastern borderlands. Out there they didn't have things like email. They still relied on letters written on paper and bits of goat skin. Emails were easier, thought Louis, but letters were more fun to receive. Emails can't be handwritten by your mum after all. Nor can they be parcelled up with one of your dad's amazing, homemade flapjacks.

Knight Sir Louis
No 1 Clunkalot
Flying through the air
On the way to Castle Sideways

The Year of Our Llama 802
The Month of Biscuits
Day the Fourth and Seven-Eighths

Champion Trixie (aka Mum)
Chivalry Farm
Squirrel Helm

Dear Mum,

I hope you and Dad are well and that the parsnips are growing better than last year.

The double-headed dragon Borax continues to rampage across the land. I'm determined to find a way of stopping it, but the people don't always make it easy! Just today I put out two big fires. The first was in the hamlet of Strawling, where all the houses are made from straw. The second fire was in Much Kindling, where all the houses are made from sticks. I asked them why they didn't build their houses from stone, like the good folks of Stoney Standing. I explained that their stone houses got quite hot, but didn't set on fire or get blown down.

The Mayor of Strawling, Lord Hoax said, 'My friend's cousin knows a scientist who said that stones are all tiny volcanoes. Therefore, they could explode at any moment. And I'm not going to argue with my friend's cousin's scientist!'

I asked him for the scientist's name and address, but Lord Hoax had no idea, of course. They're almost as bad as the people of Little Matchstick. Now, that's a really dangerous place to live!

Right now, I'm heading back to Castle Sideways. I hope Pearlin has worked out a way to stop Borax. Lots of people have their own theories, but most of them seem very silly to me.

"Pretend the dragon isn't there and it will just disappear."

"Ask the dragon to be nicer."

"Fly inside the dragon's fiery stomach with a giant ice cube."

The last idea isn't that bad, except you'd have to get past the pointy teeth first! Anyway, to keep me going, I remind myself of what you said when I became a knight.

You said, 'You're a knight now. Your true master isn't a king or a queen or a law. It's truth itself! So, imagine that there is a question mark hanging above your head Louis. Don't just accept what people say. Ask for evidence. Question everything.'

And I said: 'Why?'

And you said: 'Exactly!'

Love to Dad and the chickens. And can you ask him to send a bumper box of flapjacks? Everyone is a big fan. Including King Burt!

Lots of love

Your son, Louis xxx

P.S. Clunkalot says hello. Here's his latest haiku.

The Lord Hoax's head
resembles his manor house.
It is stuffed with straw.

CHAPTER
WORRY

OH NO! I'VE JUST REALISED THIS IS BOOK TWO AND SOME READERS MAY NOT HAVE READ BOOK ONE!

IT DOESN'T MATTER. THIS IS A COMPLETELY DIFFERENT STORY.

OH THAT'S A RELIEF.

SO, IF WE LIKE THIS STORY WE CAN ALWAYS GO BACK AND READ THE OTHER ONE AS WELL.

YES. NO SPOILERS HERE.   BRILLIANT!

CHAPTER 7

So, here we are in Chapter Seven already. Doesn't time fly? This chapter starts at Castle Sideways.

This is Castle Sideways, capital of the kingdom of Squirrel Helm. Yes, it's a very silly name for a kingdom. There's been a petition going around to change it to something more sensible.

I VOTE FOR

- O SPONGEY TOOTOWN
- O RIDICULOUS!
- O POLEY WOLEY
- O YARBOX ON TRIPPINGTON
- O SUTTON KNEEBOX
  OR...
  YES?
  WE COULD JUST CALL
  THE KINGDOM...
- O PHILIP!
- O OTHER
  (PLEASE WRITE YOUR OWN BELOW)

Since no one can agree on a new name, the kingdom remains Squirrel Helm. And this is where Louis is champion knight (and Deputy King). The castle is currently on high alert thanks to Borax's flaming antics. So far, Borax the dragon hasn't made it as far as Castle Sideways. But each attack brings it closer and closer.

Louis is, of course, on his way back for an important meeting. Here are some of the people he's coming to see:

King Burt the Not Bad

King Burt is trying to keep calm. He does this by telling other people to do things. Things like:

YOU THERE!
START STOCKPILING
ICE CUBES.
BY ORDER OF ME.

YOU THERE!
GET THE WATER
WELLS WORKING.
BY ORDER OF ME.

YOU THERE!
BUY ME THE LATEST
GAMES CONSOLE.
HERE'S MY CREDIT CARD.

Pearlin

Pearlin, the court wizard and inventor, or "wizentor" has been trying to invent a way to stop Borax. She has a very large drawing board of ideas. Here are two of them:

THE MASSIVE SPLATTER

THE GIANT STICKY BUBBLE

Pearlin hoped to enlist the help of the world's greatest wizentor Mysto. But, unfortunately, he has (once again) disappeared. He was last seen rolling off in his wizarding school, The Wizard Inventor Technical college (TWIT for short).

How can a school roll off, you're wondering? Well, Mysto's school is fitted with giant tractor wheels. Mysto liked the idea of roaming around the kingdom so that he could look for unknown magical places in between giving lessons.

Without Mysto, apprentice Pearlin had gone back to teaching herself how to be a wizentor. She preferred it that way. She didn't always get things exactly right, but they often went BANG! Or WHOOSH! Or FLOBBER-JABBERKASPLOOCH! and that was always a lot of fun. One of her more successful inventions was the new castle alarm system. It was an adapted gargoyle that sat on the top of the hill. She called it the Klaxongoyle. (It was much more effective than the prototype which was just a swan with a bell.)

As the sun vanished beneath the horizon, the Klaxongoyle sounded! A normal alarm would have gone:

BLARRRRRRT! Or WOOOOOO!

But the Klaxongoyle went:

OI! YOU LOT! THERE'S SOMEFING COMING! WATCH OUT! OI! YOU LISTENIN TO ME? WAKE UP, YOU LAZY BUNCH! COR BLIMEY!

Here's Pearlin's science report on the Klaxongoyle:

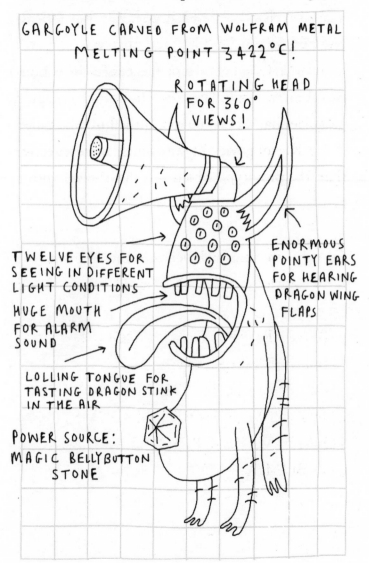

GARGOYLE CARVED FROM WOLFRAM METAL
MELTING POINT 3422°C!

ROTATING HEAD
FOR 360°
VIEWS!

TWELVE EYES FOR
SEEING IN DIFFERENT
LIGHT CONDITIONS

ENORMOUS
POINTY EARS
FOR HEARING
DRAGON WING
FLAPS

HUGE MOUTH
FOR ALARM
SOUND

LOLLING TONGUE FOR
TASTING DRAGON STINK
IN THE AIR

POWER SOURCE:
MAGIC BELLYBUTTON
STONE

King Burt and Pearlin rushed to the windows and peered out to see what was coming. Here are two possibilities:

a) A massive two-head fire-breathing dragon called Borax

b) Knight Sir Louis and Clunkalot

Head to Chapter Eight to find out which one it is.

CHAPTER 8

It was (b) Knight Sir Louis and Clunkalot.

Phew! What a relief!

The crescent moon was shining in the sky like a very large, silver toenail clipping. Knight Sir Louis sat in the Great Hall of Castle Sideways with King Burt and Pearlin.

'What are we going to do?' asked King Burt. 'All this dragon business is really getting in the way of my fun. I don't have time to play computer games anymore.'

'I've got an idea,' said Pearlin. 'What if we all move to the other side of the world?'

'Sounds a lot like running away,' said King Burt.

'Sounds better than being barbecued,' said Pearlin.

'You have a point,' agreed the king.

'I have another plan,' said Louis. 'It's time I faced and fought the dragon. I'm a knight after all. I've got Clunkalot. He can fly just like a dragon can. And I've got Dave the magic sword. He can swallow dragon fire and spit it out again.'

'But this isn't an ordinary dragon,' said Pearlin. 'This one has two heads and you only have one sword!'

King Burt tried to help: 'Maybe Pearlin can make a remote-controlled knight? Or two! Then we could send them instead.'

'How long would that take?' asked Louis.

'Hmm,' said Pearlin, working it out in her head, 'Well, I think I could have them ready in about three years.'

'THREE YEARS!' barked King Burt. 'We'll all be dragon toast by then!'

'No,' said Louis, 'I'll go. And I'll go tomorrow. It's my duty as Champion and Deputy King of Castle Sideways. It's time for a head-to-head face-to-face battle.'

'Technically,' said Pearlin, 'it'll be a head-to-head-and-head and face-to-face-and-face battle cos, you know, Borax has got two heads and two faces.'

Anyway, that's what they agreed. Burt and Louis yawned and headed to their beds. But Pearlin stayed up late fitting Clunkalot with some water cannons (hidden in his nostrils). She also fitted his eyes with some scanning sensors so he could do X-rays and find hot spots. Finally, she installed a magical emergency key. She left Louis a note about it.

Wotcher Louis.

This is an emergency key.

It took me a couple of months to get all the magic into it. If you get into big, big trouble, just turn the key and WHOOSH you'll be magically transported back to Castle Sideways. It'll only work once, right, and then I'll have to spend ages filling it up again. So only use if you really need it.
P.S. I don't know if it'll work because I haven't tested it.
Fingers crossed, yeah? P

King Burt went to bed hopeful that the nightmare of Borax would soon be over. He was starting to wonder if having his bedroom at the top of the castle was such a good idea. A dragon could easily blow fire in through his window! Perhaps he should have his things moved into one of the dungeons?

After Louis, Pearlin and King Burt had all left the Great Hall, something shifted about high up in the beams. Something had been spying on them. Now it swept down. It was . . .

. . . a flying eyeball.

The flying eyeball flew out of the nearest window and back home . . . to Castle Round-the-Twist.

CHAPTER 9

Meanwhile, Knight Sir Merry-Jingles and Queen Incredulous had started spending a lot of time together. The fact was, they had fallen madly in love. They went everywhere together . . . and even though they spent all day together, they

still scribbled little love letters to one another.
Like this:

Dear Queen of my Heart,
  Oh Queen of my head,
    Queen of my arms and legs,
  of my socks, and basically
        everything...

I love you more than anything.
More than my hat that jingles. More than
my squirting flower. Yes, even more than
jokes about botty burps. That is how
much I love thee!
        Your Knight. Your Jester
            Your Merry-Jingles

And like this:

Dear Sweet Champion,
   you are the most wonderful
   person I have ever met, because

1. you agree with all my thoughts while
   others call them 'totally ridiculous'

2. you are easy to find when I need you
   because of your tinkling bells.

3. you do as you're told

   I will love you forever, or at least
   until I have you executed or thrown into
   prison,
         Your Queen of Hearts
         (And your actual Queen
               - dont forget that!)

To begin with, people in the kingdom were happy because the Queen became distracted by her new love. But things didn't stay comfortable for long. The queen and Merry-Jingles were becoming jealous. Not of each other. But of King Burt and his champion, Knight Sir Louis.

Borax hadn't just been burning up villages in Squirrel Helm. He'd also set fire to villages in other kingdoms, including Klaptrap. Just last week, he'd set fire to the village of Ticktockboom. But the queen hadn't bothered to send out the fire brigade. Why? Well . . . mainly because she'd imprisoned the fire brigade. They'd been found eating toast. And as anyone who's read Queen Incredulous' special rules knows: toast is evil.

With no champion knight willing to save the day and with no fire brigade, the people of Klaptrap had started to worry. They had started whispering things. And Queen Incredulous had been listening in (she had some flying ears as well as some flying eyeballs).

'King Burt really cares for his people,' some said.

'Knight Sir Louis is so brave, saving people from all those fires,' others said.

'I like bananas and custard,' said some others.

The Queen and Merry-Jingles got wind of these whisperings.

'What is a banana?' asked the Queen.

'Is that the important thing, my loving majesty?' said Merry-Jingles.

'You're right,' said the Queen. 'The important thing is the custard.'

'I mean, the problem is, my love, that your subjects think King Burt is a better ruler than you.'

'And that's not the only problem, is it, sweetie?' said the queen. 'They also prefer Knight Sir Louis to you.'

They both felt very irritated. Here is a graph showing popularity ratings.

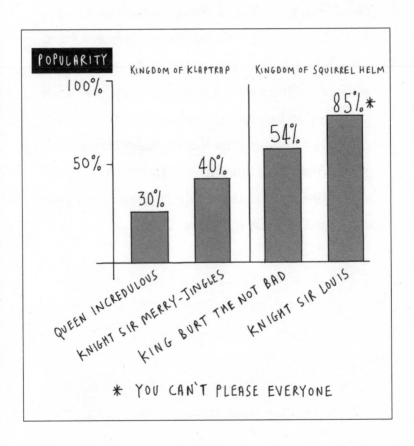

POPULARITY

KINGDOM OF KLAPTRAP   KINGDOM OF SQUIRREL HELM

100% ┐

85%*

54%

50% ┤

40%

30%

QUEEN INCREDULOUS
KNIGHT SIR MERRY-JINGLES
KING BURT THE NOT BAD
KNIGHT SIR LOUIS

* YOU CAN'T PLEASE EVERYONE

They both agreed the problem was Borax. Some smaller places, like the Land of Proud Fidget and the principality of Plopp, had been so impressed by Squirrel Helm's response that they'd put themselves under the protection of King Burt. Some people in Klaptrap had started whispering that they should do the same. When Queen Incredulous heard about this, she went green with envy. Then red with anger. Then blue with forgetting to breathe.

She's still holding her breath. Still holding. Still going. Yes. She's holding it (until we get to the next chapter apparently). I don't know about you, but it's making me feel dizzy. Ugh!

CHAPTER 10

'But,' explained Queen Incredulous, taking a deep breath, 'imagine what might happen if this Borax was defeated, not by Sir Louis. . . but by my own good Sir Merry-Jingles.'

Sir Merry-Jingles turned pale with fear. 'But I don't know the first thing about fighting dragons! I could tell it some jokes, but I've got a feeling that might end badly. Especially for me.'

'But whoever destroys the dragon will be a hero.' said the queen. 'I might even make them my king.'

'Oh! King Merry-Jingles?' he whispered to himself. He liked the sound of that.

'People of all kingdoms would admire us,' said the queen. 'They might let us rule them instead of King Burt! We'd create a new empire!'

'Emperor Merry-Jingles?' he whispered to himself. He liked the sound of that even more!

And then he had a nasty idea. And the idea grew into a scheme. Which turned into a full-blown plan. Which turned into a funny song. He was still the court jester after all, as well as the champion knight.

Oh! Flibberty Jibberty Noo!
Oh! Jingerly Jangerly Jor!
Here's my simply amazing plan
to become an EMPEROR!

Step one is to find Sir Lou
and follow wherever he goes.
I'll keep well out of his view,
but find out all that he knows!

Step two is wait for the fight
and hope that Louis's not tired
so, when Borax battles the knight,
the dragon will soon be expired!

Step three. Get Louis to chat
and say, "So glad that you won."
Then clonk him hard on his hat
till he forgets what he's done.

Step four is to seek promotion
by claiming, "I got the lizard."
I'll soon have people's devotion
from peasant right up to wizard!

Step five is to kick out the kings.
Our plans will soon be complete.
We'll grab all their precious things,
lie back and put up our feet.

Queen Incredulous listened to the song. She liked it a lot.

Knight Sir Merry-Jingles left that very night. He and the queen promised to write gooey love letters to one another every day.

Sir Merry-Jingles went to the stables to choose a horse. It was then he realised he had never ridden a real horse. He hadn't the faintest idea how to even get on a horse. They looked very tall and a bit scary. That's when he remembered one of his favourite jester props. Hobson his hobby horse!

He rode off (jingling) into the night. But only on two legs. And not very fast.

CHAPTER HOT

Normally Chapter Ten is followed by Chapter Eleven, but not today. Today it is followed by Chapter Hot and you'll find out why very soon. It's time to see a real knight in action!

Louis had woken early, nervous about the big day. Would he defeat the dragon and save the world? Or would Borax have the last laugh? (Technically, it would be the last two laughs since Borax had two heads.) Louis didn't feel like eating breakfast. His tummy felt all bubbly. But he did eat eggs, beans and crumpets (again) because he knew he needed all the energy he could get. At last, he climbed onto Clunkalot to the cheers of his friends and waved goodbye. Clunkie had prepared a little poem to cheer him up.

YOU FEAR THE WASP'S STING
BUT BESIDE THE GREAT DRAGON
YOU ARE THE WASP'S STING

'Hey, thanks, Clunkie,' said Louis. It made him feel a little better. 'Let's go!'

Clunkalot flicked out his retractable wings and swept them both up into the sky above Castle Sideways. Louis felt his sword clanking softly against his armour. He reminded himself, he wasn't alone. He had Clunkie and he had his magic sword Dave, or to give his sword its full name . . . Senator Jibber Jabber Ticket Flick It Sprocket Wicket Dingle David.

Dave had all kinds of special features. He'd been forged using the remains of a magic mirror. He could do all kinds of great things like . . . well here's a list of some of them that Louis keeps on a notelet on his fridge door.

DAVE ABSORBS FIREBOLTS, BOUNCES THEM INSIDE HIS MIRROR BLADE, AND SHOOTS THEM OUT AGAIN! WOW!

DAVE CANNOT BE HELD BY ANYONE EVIL! FACT.

DAVE SINGS WHEN THE WIND BLOWS ACROSS HIS SHARP EDGE. SOUNDS AWFUL UNLESS YOU'RE A WALRUS.

Louis had grabbed a map of Dooooooom from the castle stores before he'd left. Now he unfurled it and realised it was useless. Few that had travelled to Doooooom had returned. The map showed the border between the two lands. The hills and rivers and towns were marked on the Squirrel Helm side. But on the Doooooom side there was nothing except for a note saying, 'Please fill this in if you're passing. Cheers. And maybe take a fireproof suit.'

Louis watched the world pass by below as they flew. The green plains and forests of Squirrel Helm were pocked with smooth, limestone hills that, from up here, looked like pebbles dropped in the ground from a great height. The land looked so beautiful and cheery. Louis almost forgot he was on his way to fight a fire-breathing, evil dragon. Almost. But soon he spotted charred buildings. And then the green grass gave way to sand and rocks and then he flew out of the land of Squirrel Helm and on towards Doooooom.

Louis took a deep breath. The air smelled different here. Like bins. On fire. Ugh! He passed over a red river and then, on the other side, he spied great, lumbering shapes.

Dragons.

Some even looked up at him, the passing thing in the sky. But they didn't seem bothered. What possible threat could it be to them?

Louis could feel the time for battle was near. He hated all the waiting. He just wanted to get it done! He felt nervous. His tummy rumbled. He did a little fart.

Pffff

'Sorry about that, Clunkie!' said Louis. 'Anyway, can you look for dragons with two heads?'

Clunkie switched on his new thermal sensors to scan the land of Doooooom. Sure enough, he soon spotted a dragon with two long necks, snoozing at the entrance to a huge cave.

'Looks like Borax,' said Louis. 'Take us in, Clunkie! Here goes! Things are about to get a lot hotter!'

CHAPTER
HOTTER

Now, imagine you're Borax the dragon for a moment. This is tricky to imagine as you'll need two brains! Anyway, . . . you're snoozing the morning away, feeling very satisfied with all the chaos you've caused. It's made you feel very powerful. You remind yourself that nothing and no one can stop you doing whatever you want. Ever. You're planning your next raid. Perhaps you should set fire to one of those castles? Castle Sideways or Castle Round-the-Twist?

Just then you notice a sparkle of something in the clouds above and you look up. Whatever it is . . . it's coming your way. What is it?

A bird?

A box?

No.

It's a metal horse.

With wings!

What?

Now, imagine you're someone else . . . medieval sports commentator Eleanor Croquet-Boules. You've spent a week at the International Silly Face Tournament, where people from all over the world have gathered to contort their faces into the strangest shapes.

After all that nonsense, you really want to do something a bit more thrilling. And now's your chance. You get to commentate on the battle between Knight Sir Louis and the dragon Borax.

TRUST ME, FOLKS, THINGS ARE ABOUT TO HEAT UP HERE.

YARGL AND SCABA DON'T HANG ABOUT! FIRE BOLTS ARE COMING FROM BOTH MOUTHS. WHAT CAN LOUIS DO ABOUT THAT?

OH AMAZING! LOUIS HAS SPUN CLONKALOT INTO A TWISTING FREEFALL.

BUT HERE COMES ANOTHER FIRE BOLT!

LOUIS' MAGIC SWORD DAVE HAS EATEN IT UP AND SPAT IT BACK!

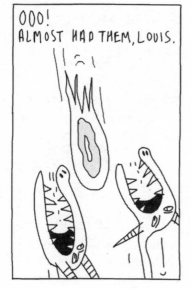

OOO! ALMOST HAD THEM, LOUIS.

WHOA! LOUIS IS FLYING LOW! WHAT'S HE UP TO? MY GUESS! TRYING TO GET BORAX TO SMASH INTO SOMETHING!

WHOA! BORAX HARDLY SLOWING DOWN THERE. JUST EXTRAORDINARY.

CRASH!

AND AS THE CHASE GOES ON, HERE ARE A FEW STATISTICS ABOUT THIS MATCH. SIR LOUIS IS KNOWN FOR HIS CALM, CLEAR THINKING BRAIN. THAT'S ONLY ONE BRAIN. BORAX IS KNOWN FOR HIS AND HER SCHEMING BRAINS. THAT'S TWO BRAINS. SO, BORAX DEFINITELY HAS THE ADVANTAGE THERE. THAT'S DOUBLE THE THINKY TIME. OF COURSE, SIR LOUIS DOES ALSO HAVE CLUNKALOT'S ROBOT BRAIN. AND PERHAPS THE SWORD DAVE HAS SOME SORT OF MIND TOO. WE'RE NOT REALLY SURE! BUT HERE'S THE CRUCIAL FACTOR FOLKS... YARGL AND SCABA'S BRAINS ARE CONNECTED AND CAN WORK TOGETHER. I DON'T THINK THAT'S HOW IT WORKS FOR LOUIS AND CLUNKIE.

71

WHOA! LOUIS HAS SWUNG ABOUT FOR A FULL-FRONTAL ASSAULT. COULD THIS BE HIS MOMENT OF GLORY?

IF IT IS VICTORY FOR LOUIS, THEN THE BOOK WOULD PROBABLY END HERE. SO THAT'S A CLUE, RIGHT?

CHAPTER HOTTEST

It was a clue.

Knight Sir Louis flew straight towards Borax. His only hope of victory was to destroy both heads at once. His only way to survive the dragon fire was to capture every fire bolt sent at him inside his magic sword Dave. If he missed just one it would be toastie time.

Scaba blasted out three bolts of fire. Yargl blasted out four! Louis swung Dave around expertly. Caught them in the magical blade . . . one, two, three, four . . . span Clunkie upside down and hung on . . . five, six . . .

Meanwhile, inside Dave, the first bolt of dragon fire was bouncing around getting annoyed. It had been trapped inside a magical, reflective prison. It couldn't find anything to blow up or set on fire. Then the other fire bolts joined the first and pinged around together. Dave's magic could easily cope with one or two of these. But six! Dave the sword started to feel unwell.

TEPID
WARM
HOT
SCALDING

'Oh no,' thought Dave. 'I'm starting to feel a bit melty.'

Sir Louis felt Dave's hilt getting suddenly hot and he instinctively let go of the sword. Dave fell to the ground and burped. Six fire bolts rushed out of him and bounced off into a nearby cave.

BOOM!
CRASH!
BLAST! KABLAM!
PLOCK! SINGE!

OI! THAT WAS MY CAVE THAT WAS. I JUST FINISHED DECORATING IT AND ALL. WHAT'VE I EVER DONE TO YOU? TSK! TYPICAL!

Meanwhile the seventh fire bolt was still on course and heading for Louis and Clunkie. This is the sort of time when most people go, 'AGHHHHHH!' But Louis stayed calm and shouted into Clunkie's aluminium ears, 'NOSE HOSE!'

Sure enough, Clunkie ejected a spurt of water at the last fire bolt.

They met and suddenly there was a huge cloud of steam!

Louis and Clunkalot were flying blind. Louis had no idea where Borax was. Fortunately, Borax also had no idea where Louis was.

Phew!

But the phew didn't last for long.

Louis emerged from the cloud, flying between Borax's necks and over their long body. Borax was swift and turned to take another shot at the pesky knight and his tin can horse. Louis made a dash for the ground. He had to retrieve Dave!

Now, this is where a lot of knights would get things totally wrong. They'd think, I'm a big, brave knight. It's a horrible dragon. I'm bound to win because I'm the good guy. This kind of sloppy thinking leads to a missing knight and a dragon sleeping off a big meal.

But Louis isn't that sort of a knight.

He had already decided Borax was too quick, too cunning and too dangerous. It was time to retreat and come up with a new plan. On a danger scale of one to ten Borax was about a forty-two.

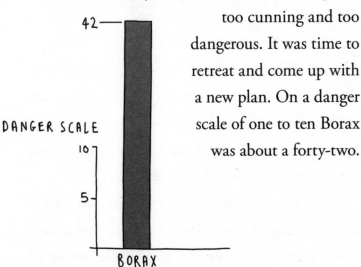

Louis rushed for his sword. Borax saw where he was headed. And the two brains of Scaba and Yargl immediately agreed on a terrible idea. As one they both breathed fire. The two bolts of blue dragon fire rushed forwards at the same time. They combined into one enormous flower of flame. Surely Louis didn't stand a chance!

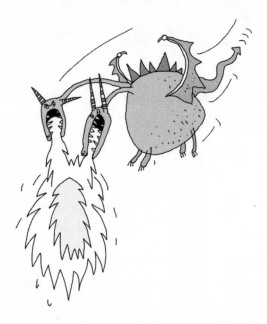

Sir Louis flew down to his sword. Reached. Grabbed it and flung himself inside Clunkie's belly. Just as the flames were about to melt them all . . . Louis fitted and twisted Pearlin's emergency key.

A micro-second later Clunkie vanished! The flames of Borax hit just where he'd been. Borax assumed the pesky knight and his horse had been vaporised. Scaba and Yargl smiled nastily at each other and settled down for a snooze.

Anyway, that is the end of Chapters Hot, Hotter and Hottest. A very hot series of chapters I'm sure you'll agree. Even hotter than Chapters One and Five and they were boiling!

Meanwhile . . .

COR. PHEW. THIS IS EXHAUSTING! RIGHT, HOBSON? PHEW!

CHAPTER 11

Pearlin's emergency spell had worked! When Louis turned Pearlin's emergency key, Clunkie, Louis and Dave vanished and reappeared . . . where? Louis looked out of the hatch in the side of Clunkie.

WE'LL HAVE TO EAT OUR WAY IN!
JUST NEED TO ORGANISE A JELLY
EATING CONTEST.

They were surrounded by something thick and wobbly that smelled faintly of blackcurrant.

In fact, they were outside Castle Sideways. But the spell had had an unexpected side effect. Clunkie was trapped inside an enormous cube of thick jelly.

Louis had some time to kill while Pearlin and the castle courtiers ate the enormous jelly cube. 'Clunkie, let me see your scans from the battle.'

Clunkie's sensors had taken a perfect X-ray of the dragon. Louis studied it carefully.

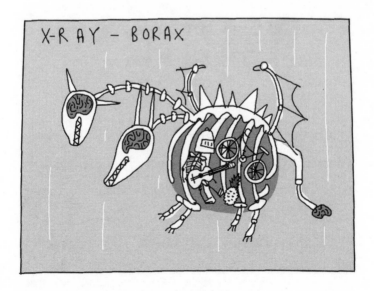

There was quite a lot of junk inside the dragon. Bits of knight's armour and some cow bells and nose rings and unpleasant things like that. But Louis noticed something else strange. He saw the shadows indicating the two brains of Yargl and Scaba. But there was a third shadow, similar, but half the size. A third brain! It sat right at the end of the tail.

About an hour later Pearlin and the castle courtiers had eaten a channel through the jelly cube and it fell apart in two big slabs.

SPLONGE. FLOMP.

'Thanks, Pearlin,' said Louis, 'your emergency key saved us.'

'Good to know,' she said. 'Shame about the jelly thing. Weird.'

As Pearlin took back the key she said, 'Better get it charged up with some more magic juice. Probably take a month.'

Just then King Burt came rushing out, 'There you are. Oh, I say! Sir Louis! You're still alive. Does this mean you defeated Borax?'

'I'm afraid not, your majesty,' said Louis, 'I think we're going to need some professional help.'

'Oh!' said King Burt. 'You mean like dragon cleaners? People that come in, look for dragons, sweep them up into a bag and put them in the dustbin? That sort of thing?'

'Not really, your majesty,' said Louis. 'Do you know anyone like that?'

'No,' said King Burt. 'But . . . maybe we could ask the Dragon Slayers of Niblet?'

'That would be an excellent idea,' said Louis, 'if they existed.'

'But they do!' said King Burt confused.

'No, my liege,' explained Louis, 'that's just your favourite computer game. It's not real.'

'Oh!' said King Burt, who liked to play games most of the day. 'I suppose I do sometimes get confused between reality and gameplay. Oh well, at least I know Herk Noodle the Hedgepig is real.'

'I'm afraid not, sir,' said Louis, 'he's also just a character in a game.'

'Really?' said King Burt. 'Are you real?'

'I think so,' said Louis poking himself.

'Splendid,' said Burt, 'Then, who are you gonna call?'

'I know,' said Pearlin, interrupting. 'It's time we found the world's greatest wizentor!'

'Exactly,' said Louis.

'Ah! Now, I know who you mean,' said Burt. 'You're talking about Mungo and Lungo the magic gargoyles of Dingleberry-Dong.'

'Er . . . no,' said Louis. 'That's yet another game, sir. We're talking about Mysto.'

'Oh yes, Mysto,' said Burt. 'Carry on!'

CHAPTER 12

Meanwhile both of Borax's heads, Yargl and Scaba, were also busy making new plans. They didn't want to do anything like take over the world, or become king and queen of this place or that. No, what they wanted was chaos. Beautiful, utter, chaos. A world where they were free to be a non-stop nuisance today, tomorrow and forever. It was too much fun!

But it was hard to cause so much chaos on their own. What they needed were some other dragons to help out. But other dragons didn't much like Borax. Some were good dragons who disapproved of Borax's menacing ways.

Others were bad dragons like them, but who were busy with their own smaller ploys.

They didn't want to get involved in Borax's schemes. And so Yargl and Scaba started a process in their own body. A process called parthenogenesis.

PARTY OF JENNY'S SIS?   ALMOST. PARTH-EN-O-GEN-E-SIS!   WHAT'S THAT THEN?

And now over to Professor Petula Petri-Dish for a short science lesson.

THIS MUMMY PYTHON HAS BEEN ON HER OWN FOR YEARS.

EVEN WITHOUT A DADDY SHE HAS LAID SOME EGGS.

Yargl and Scaba Borax laid their eggs. Soon, very soon, there would be a lot more Boraxes to deal with.

Uh-oh!

Meanwhile . . .

CHAPTER 13

Knight Sir Louis launched out from Castle Sideways in his robot horse, Clunkalot. They circled up higher and higher to get a good view of the kingdoms around them. Louis needed to find Mysto's school and quickly.

Mysto's school of magic, recently renamed the Scientific Academy of Unusual Conjuration and Enchantment (or SAUCE for short) didn't stay in one place for long.

It looked like a very boring, squarish, concrete office building. Well, almost. The school now had six giant feet and an enormous wheel under the belly of the building. It rolled around the plains, hills and valleys.

Now, quests are all about making important decisions, so, here's your chance to get involved!

From his high vantage point Louis could see two ways to go. South towards the Jabby Mountains or west towards the Lake of Klook.

If you think Louis should go to the mountains, go to **chapter 15**!

If you think Louis should go to the lake, go to **chapter 16**!

CHAPTER 14

The Bogs of Wattasmel were famous for their appalling, nose-twisting reek. Ugh! They were also famous for swallowing things up whole. Like cows, and houses, and once, a whole pirate ship (but that's another story – a story called Captain Hatch and the Double-Eye Patch). Anyway, the bogs were famous for the terrible farting noises that belched all day and all night.

BURRRRFSQUEEEE WOBBERWOBBERWOBBER PLURP

The bogs were also famous for their champion knight, Knight Sir Colin. Louis knew him well. Colin was a good friend. He was also quite a smelly friend. But then so would you be if you lived in the Bogs of Wattasmel.

Louis flew on Clunkie through the thick, stinking mists above the bogs. Clunkie switched on his headlamp eyeballs.

They searched for Colin's home which was in the boughs of an absolutely enormous tree. It was, in fact, the only tree in the bogs that hadn't rotted away to nothing. Despite its size, it was very hard to see thanks to the thick fog. Louis worried they might accidentally fly straight into it. This would be bad for at least two reasons. Number one, it would hurt. And number two, if they survived, they would fall down into the bog.

That smell just didn't wash out.

Luckily, Clunkie's headlamp eyeballs were working well, and they soon saw the great tree.

Clunkie hovered above and came in to land on Knight Sir Colin's landing pad, right next to his giant tame bat, Malcolm.

Louis looked around for his friend, but he wasn't anywhere to be seen.

'Colin? Where are you?'

A piece of mud opened its eyes and stood up. It was Colin, covered head to toe in gooey clay. Colin was chilling out in his favourite place, the Mudarium, like a big bathhouse except full of mud.

'Louis! What a pleasure to see you. Come for a mud bath, have you?'

'Er, no thanks,' said Louis.

'Don't know what you're missing,' said Colin.

'I'm looking for Mysto and his roving school. Have you seen him?' asked Louis.

'Not seen Mysto,' said Colin, 'but I know exactly where his school is.'

A short while later, they headed up to the treetop where Louis climbed onto Clunkalot and Colin jumped onto Malcolm the Bat's saddle. They flew for about twenty minutes across the bogs, then down, down, down until they came to a little rocky island sticking up out of the burping, bubbling bog. Except it wasn't a rocky island at all. It was the remains of Mysto's school on wheels.

'Looks like everyone escaped,' said Colin. 'One of the advantages of being wizards, I suppose. Though their magic didn't save the school. Once the bog starts sucking something down, nothing can stop it.'

They landed on top of the school. The extra weight made it wobble and sink a little deeper into the bog.

FLLUUUURGG

Louis jumped down from Clunkie onto the roof and grabbed some rope. 'Maybe there's a clue to where Mysto went. I'm going inside.'

'Be careful,' said Colin joining him, 'we don't want to be sucked under too!'

They found an open window and climbed inside. The room was chaos with chairs, tables and magical equipment all thrown around and broken. They looked out into the corridor which was now a long slide down into the sucking bog.

Louis tied the rope to the radiator and lowered himself down the corridor. As he passed each door, he read the words written on them.

Astrolololololology (like astrology, but with more lols)

Magical Languages (including Fadarax, Borgon and Tickelingo)

Alchemistry (like normal chemistry, but more magical)

Gymnasium (even wizards have to keep fit)

School Hamster (don't worry, she'd already been rescued)

Wizenting (inventing for wizards)

And, at last, just a few inches above the stinky, creeping bog, Headmaster Mysto's Office.

Louis pushed the door open and leapt inside. Even as he did, the school shuddered and he heard the horrible sound of the burping bog.

'Louis! Time to get out of here,' he heard Colin call from above.

Suddenly, Mysto's office filled with a strange glow. Louis turned and saw Mysto standing before him. Except it wasn't actually Mysto.

HELLO LOUIS. YOU HAVE ACTIVATED
MY HOLOGRAPHIC RECORDED MESSAGE.
WELL DONE! I EXPECT YOU'VE BEEN
LOOKING FOR ME. YOU NEED SOMETHING
TO DEFEAT THE DRAGON BORAX. WELL
THERE'S GOOD NEWS AND BAD NEWS.
THE GOOD NEWS IS I KNOW WHAT YOU
NEED. IT'S A MAGICAL OBJECT OF
GREAT POWER!

WHAT YOU'RE
LOOKING FOR
IS AN ICE
CUCUMBER!

'What? Magical vegetables again!' thought Louis. 'Well, at least it's not a potato.' (Not long ago, he'd had a lot of trouble with a potato-obsessed wizard. True story.)

IT'S SAID ITS COLD POWERS ARE AMAZING! IT CAN FREEZE ANYTHING. EVEN A VOLCANO! I'M NOT SURE IF YOU NEED THE WHOLE THING, OR JUST A SLICE, OR MAYBE YOU HAVE TO MAKE A SALAD WITH IT. I DON'T KNOW YET.

'So that's the good news,' said Mysto. 'The bad news is . . . I've no idea where to find an Ice Cucumber. And now we've got ourselves stuck in this wretched bog. Anyway, I might have found something else useful. I'm heading back to the

Jabby Mountains after we abandon the school. We were there a few weeks ago and something strange happened.'

Before Louis could hear any more, the school lurched and the dreaded bog mud started leaking into the room. Louis leapt to the door frame and reached for the rope.

'PULL!' he shouted to Colin, who heaved Louis up as fast as he could.

Even as Colin heaved, the school slipped deeper into the mud.

Louis reached the top and they both scrambled up and out of the window and onto the backs of Malcolm and Clunkalot.

With a flap of their wings, the two steeds rose into the mist and Colin and Louis looked down as the school disappeared beneath the bog surface.

If you think Louis should stop jumping around chapters like this, go to **chapter 17**!

If you think Louis should go to the Lake of Klook to see what else he can discover, go to **chapter 16**!

CHAPTER 15

The Jabby Mountains were so-called because they were very pointy. The peaks were jabby. The boulders were jabby. Even the pebbles were pretty jabby. *Jab jab jab*.

Louis asked Clunkalot to use his telescopic eyeballs to find Mysto's mysterious, movable school. Clunkie saw something on one of the mountainsides and flew down for a closer look.

Louis hopped off and ran over. Sure enough, there were tracks made by the roaming school. But the tracks were old.

'Looks like it was here, but a while ago,' he said. Then he noticed some rocks piled up against the bottom of one cliff. He walked over for a better look. Maybe they were important somehow? But the nearer he got to the clump of rocks the harder it was to remember what he was doing there.

He stood there a while thinking to himself, 'What am I doing here?'

Then he walked back to Clunkie. He noticed the pile of rocks again.

'Ah yes!' he thought. 'I was going to check out that strange pile of rocks.'

WHAT AM I DOING HERE?

And over he wandered once more. And once again, the closer he got the harder it was to remember what he was doing there.

He stood there a while thinking to himself.

After half an hour of going back and forth, Louis sat down on the rocks and stayed there.

Clunkie started to get worried. He was sure something strange was going on. It wasn't normal for Louis to just sit around doing nothing. Clunkie decided he should walk over to check on his master. He took a couple of steps towards Louis and changed his mind. He didn't like those rocks. Now he was a little nearer, he could hear something coming from amongst the rubble. It was very high pitched. He used his special robot brain to listen and slow it down. It was a voice. It was saying: **'Forget everything. Forget. Forget. Forget all that you know. Forget. Be nice to rocks. Remember that bit, but everything else. Forget. Forget.'**

Clunkie didn't know what was causing it and didn't want to find out. So he extended his grappling hook and dragged Louis back.

'Thanks, Clunkie,' said Louis, looking a bit confused. 'What was all that about?'

Clunkie produced a printed poem for Louis.

SOMETIMES THE ANSWER
TO THE ROCKIEST QUESTION
ARRIVES LATER ON

'Interesting,' said Louis. 'You're right. A quest for another day. We need to find the school. And be nice to rocks . . . eh? What?!'

And they set off again, flying high. Louis looked around. He could see the Lake of Klook to the northwest. And to the northeast were the Bogs of Wattasmel.

If you think Louis should go to the bogs, go to **chapter 14**!

If you think Louis should head off to the lake, go to **chapter 16**!

CHAPTER 16

The Lake of Klook is not a beautiful place. But then, it's not an ugly place either. It's just, sort of, all right. Bland. The grass is a greyish sort of green. The sky is a greyish sort of blue. And the rocks are a greyish sort of . . . well . . . grey.

Louis was starting to feel a bit peckish, so he picked a grey fruit from a grey branch and took a bite. It tasted of absolutely nothing. Then Louis realised, he couldn't smell anything. He took deep breaths in through his nose. Nope! The Lake of Klook had no smell.

'Well, Clunkie. I think this is the most boring place I've ever been,' said Louis.

'And that's why I like it,' said someone.

Louis spun around. Sitting on a rock in the lake

was a mermaid. She had a shock of electric blue hair, and around her neck a strange necklace of neon-lipped shells.

'Hiya, I'm Sonya,' the mermaid said. 'They call me Sonya the Shoe Eater.'

'That's an interesting name,' said Louis. 'Why do they call you that?'

'Because I eat shoes,' said Sonya.

'Right,' said Louis, who'd been hoping it was some sort of metaphor.

'Not that I've had one for ages,' said Sonya. 'It's all lake snakes, duckweed and crawlyfish here.'

'If you don't like it here,' said Louis, 'I'm sure I can drop you off at a shoe shop.'

'Oh, I do like it here,' said Sonya. 'You see I'm a hermit. I like being on my own. I don't really like excitement. So, this place is ideal. Except for the lack of shoes.'

'Yes,' said Louis. 'Er. Anyway! I don't suppose you've seen a wizentor by the name of Mysto? Or a school on wheels?'

'Funny you should say that,' said Sonya. 'There was a big building like that here a while back. Stopped on the lake shore. This little guy spent ages fishing in the waters, looking for something.'

'Mysto was here, then,' said Louis to Clunkie. 'I wonder what he was looking for?'

'Oh, he was probably looking for one of these,' said Sonya, pointing to her neon shell necklace.

'A shell? But what's so special about a shell?'

'These aren't just ordinary shells. These are light keys to the water kingdom of Turbot.'

'Oh! They sound good,' said Louis. 'Would you give me one of the shells? I could pass it on to

Mysto when I see him. I'm sure if he was looking for it, he had a good reason.'

'I'm sorry. There's nothing you could give me in exchange for my shells,' said Sonya and she turned, ready to dive back into the water. 'I'm going to go now. I've not spoken to anyone for years, and I really don't enjoy it. Sorry. I don't mean to be rude.'

'What about a shoe?' blurted out Louis before she could dive.

Sonya turned. 'What's that?'

'Would you give me one of your shells in exchange for a tasty shoe?'

Louis reached inside Clunkie and pulled out two large, soft and well-worn slippers. Sonya's eyes almost popped out on stalks. She started salivating.

'Oh! Shoes. Tasty, stinky old shoes. Delicious!'

Sonya swam over, eyes agog, and handed over a neon-lipped shell in exchange for the slippers.

'Oh, go on then,' she said. 'Just this once.'

And she took the slippers and dived under the lake surface.

'What a strange day this is turning out to be,' said Louis. He looked at the beautiful shell. 'I hope it was worth it,' he said to Clunkie. 'I really liked those slippers.'

Louis and Clunkie flew off to continue their search for Mysto.

Over to the east, Louis could see the mist rising over the Bogs of Wattasmel. To the south, he could see loads more chapters and, well, the rest of this book.

If you think Louis should visit the bogs, go to **chapter 14**!

If you think Louis should go south and, you know, just get on with the story, go to **chapter 17**. (But you should probably check out **chapter 14**. Just saying!)

Meanwhile . . .

CHAPTER 17

Okay! Enough of that jumping around!

Let's get on with the story.

Thanks to Chapter Fourteen (did you read that one?) Louis now knew what he had to find to defeat the dragon Borax. He had to find something called an Ice Cucumber! It didn't sound very dangerous. In fact, it sounded very silly indeed. But it did have the word ice in it, which was probably the important bit, considering how hot and fiery Borax was.

AND THANKS TO CHAPTER SIXTEEN
(DID YOU READ THAT ONE TOO?)
HE NOW HAD A NEON-LIPPED SHELL
THAT WAS BOUND TO COME IN
HANDY SOMETIME.

YEAH, YEAH,
WE KNOW!

But where did you get things like Ice Cucumbers? wondered Louis. Even Mysto didn't seem to know. He was going to have to find somebody who knew things about magical salad.

Fortunately, his best friend Mr Catalogue was due to graduate from the famous University of Hogford that very afternoon with a degree in Weird Botany.

CHAPTER 18

Here is the prospectus for the University of Hogford.

Hogford has the richest history of any university in all the kingdoms. Founded a thousand years ago when Hogford was just a large, slippery pig farm, it has gone from strength to strength.

The legend goes that a magical accident turned nine of the pigs into great thinkers, including the smartest amongst them, Tractorina Swill. Working together, the smart pigs convinced the farmers, the

Orwells, that they should be allowed to manage the farm themselves. It is said the Orwells listened carefully, and then ran off shouting, 'Agh! Agh! The pigs are talking! Agh!' Soon after the university's first chancellor, Tractorina, was appointed.

Today, the University of Hogford is still recognised as one of the best places to study, whether you are a pig, human, elf, dwarf, troll, ogre, or tree. Some of its most popular courses include *Ludicrous Chemistry*, *Advanced Goblin Dentistry*, and languages such as *Southern Trollish* and *Ancient Mermish*.

CHAPTER 19

Sir Louis and Clunkie flew towards the pretty town of Hogford, following the flow of the River Burble. Before long the beautiful old college buildings came into view. Louis checked the address. Mr Catalogue was studying at Saint Trotter's College. It was one of the smaller buildings, though it was also one of the oldest too. In fact, it had been built on the site of the original Hogford Farm.

Louis found Room 19 and knocked for Mr Catalogue.

A FEW FACTS ABOUT
MR CATALOGUE

FIRST NAME: DOESN'T HAVE ONE

MIDDLE NAME: MILDRED

SURNAME: CATALOGUE

INTELLIGENCE: HIGH

MR CATALOGUE WAS TRANSFORMED FROM A NORMAL, SNUFFLING CHOMPING BOAR INTO A 'MUCH MORE THINKY' BOAR BY AN EVIL WIZARD UP TO NO GOOD.

OTHER COMMENTS: MR CATALOGUE IS ACTUALLY A LADY.

Mr (no name) Mildred Catalogue opened the door and gave Louis a big, clanking hug. (Trotters hugging armour will make a clank.)

'Long time, no seeing!' said Mr Catalogue.

'But I saw you last Wednesday,' said Louis.

'Yeah, true-ish,' said Mr Catalogue, 'apart from I've been a-studying in the Room of Frozen Time. So, for me, six old years have gone zip-zip-zip since I last saw you.'

'Wow!' said Louis. 'That's a lot of studying.'

'I knows it,' said Mr Catalogue. 'I gone and passed my course in Weird Botany, plus I did the chunky advanced course, and also the supers advanced mega wow-wow course.'

'That's astonishing! Well done.'

'I evens did a night school for some languages too. I has learned a bit of Ogre. I'm not that good and all, but I reckon I could do an order off a menu.'

'I'm proud of you, Mr Catalogue,' said Louis.

Mr Catalogue held up a trotter to stop him.

'And that's another good wotsit. Now I is so qualified, I don't have to calls meself mister no more.

MENU

FOR BREAKFAST TODAY WE
HAVE OGRISH SPECIALS INCLUDING:

Sssskkrrurggggg
CHOMBR EGGS SERVED WITH LASHING OF YURKELB

HONKERY
EVERYONE'S FAVOURITE

FURTELNARGISHYBONG
THIS WEEK'S SPECIAL

Td
GET IT WHILE IT'S FRESH

FLONb
POACHED, SMASHED OR BURNT

Rrrr
WITH TtttsURG'S MILK

'You're a professor already?!' said Louis smiling hopefully.

'Not quites!' laughed the boar. 'I is what's called a Reader.'

'Oh, well done!'

'So, now you gets to call me Reader Catalogue.'

'Nice one, Reader!' said Louis. 'I mean, it's a bit confusing with your surname being what it is, but still, well done.'

Louis and Catalogue headed to the canteen for lunch. Louis told her all about the Ice Cucumber.

'Aw, no!' said Catalogue. 'Not that word! I always ends up saying koom-bar-bar or koo-mumber.'

'The big problem is where to find one,' explained Louis. 'I've asked around, but no one's heard of such a thing.'

'We needs to look it up in the library. They've got a hooooooge one here in Hogford. Some of them books there are older than rocks.'

'Sounds good,' said Louis. Just then, he spotted the painting of the university's founder on the wall. Tractorina herself.

'I guess you chose this place because of her,' said Louis pointing at the painting.

'That's right,' said Catalogue, 'she's totally me hero. If only I had some time shoes, I'd go back and shake her trotters and say you is awesomey.'

'Well, if we ever find the wizentor Mysto again,' said Louis, 'you can ask him to make a pair for you.'

CHAPTER 20

The library was brand new.

The old library had been stuffed so full of books that there wasn't any room left for people. So, a famous architect, Lisabet Splott, had been asked to build a new one. Actually, she'd won a competition. Here's a clipping from the The *Hogford Herald*.

Before we reveal the winning entry of the new library building competition, here are a few of the entries that didn't make it with the judges' comments.

The Big Book (too obvious)

The Tall Tower (too many stairs)

The Cactus (too prickly)

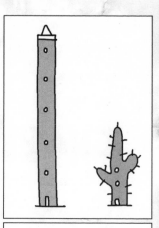

The Spaceship (too spaceshippy)

The Pyramid (not enough windows – in fact, NO windows)

And now, we can reveal Splott's winning design.

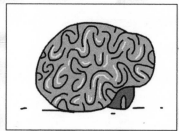

Are you thinking what I'm thinking? If it's *ugh!* then you are.

Yes, the new library was shaped like a huge, knobbly, pink brain. They'd even managed to make it glisten as though it was gooey and wet. Ew!

It looked disgusting, but was very hard to miss. Everyone knew exactly where the library was. Inside, as you'd expect, were rows and rows of books.

In most libraries, books are organised alphabetically by subject. But not here. Splott had also decided to organise the books by colour and shade. There was a floor of red books, a floor of blue books, a floor of yellow books and so on. This meant the inside of the library looked quite beautiful, like being inside a rainbow.

Unfortunately, it also meant it was almost impossible to find the book you were looking for. A huge team of librarians had to be employed to remember where the books were.

Louis and Catalogue entered the building and approached a librarian.

'Hey Argie!' said Catalogue. 'How's it going?'

The librarian, a young, eager cyclops, smiled and said, 'Hi Catalogue. We still on for our Hogford sandwich crawl?'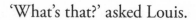

'What's that?' asked Louis.

'Oh, it's the sort of thing students is doing,' explained Catalogue, 'visiting a bunch of different sandwich shoppies one after the other until you're really stuffed. And yes, Argie, I'm definitely coming.'

Argie was Catalogue's best friend at the university. Argie had been a student at the university (studying Advanced Pickle Making) before pursuing his other passion, books. Now, he was an assistant librarian. Catalogue had met Argie in her first week and they'd bonded over a shared love of bread rolls, pickled eggs and fairy tales.

'This here is my old mate, Knight Sir Louis,' explained Catalogue.

'Very pleased to meet you,' said Louis.

'Wow, a real knight,' said Argie. 'How can I help?'

'We're looking for a book on koombarbars,' explained Catalogue.

'Cucumbers? Hmm,' said Argie looking around at the rainbow of books. 'I can try. But no promises. I have about a twenty percent success rate but that's up on last month.'

Eventually, Argie led them to a row of dark blue books. 'I think it might be here . . . somewhere.'

They split up and each checked a third of the books' spines. They included:

THE ADVENTURES OF SAMUEL THE SWORDFISH BY TIFFY WING

MY WAY OR THE HIGHWAY BY QUEEN INCREDULOUS

WHY WEDNESDAYS SHOULD BE BANNED BY BOB TUESDAY

MEDIUM SIZED EXPECTATIONS BY DARLES CHICKENS

CHERRY PLOPPER AND THE GASTROLOGER'S GROAN BY C.K. TOWELING

Then, at last, after about five hours of searching, Argie spotted what they were looking for:

PROFESSOR TRISH
WILDING'S GUIDE
TO
MYSTICAL
FRUIT AND VEGETABLES

AS RECOMMENDED IN
MONSTER VEGETABLE MAGAZINE

'What a relief,' said Argie with a big smile. 'See you later!' And he headed off to help the next poor customer.

Louis and Catalogue flicked to the back of the book and found a picture index.

'Has it got koombarbars in it?' asked Catalogue.

'Yes,' replied Louis. 'Loads!'

They turned to the page for Ice Cucumbers and Louis read:

The Ice Cucumber is the rarest of all mystical cucumbers. In fact, it is one of the rarest of all mystical fruits and vegetables, except perhaps for the Prune of Destiny and of course the Rhubarb of Small Curses.

The Ice Cucumber does not grow where you might expect to find it – that is – the far north or far south in the icy poles. No! In fact, it grows in another very cold place: the depths of the ocean. It grows where there is no light, or at least, no normal light. Magical rays of light do penetrate to the deepest ocean floor. This magical light is the only light that helps the Ice Cucumbers grow, and perhaps explains their amazing and dangerous powers. The Ice Cucumber is quite safe to touch, but must never be eaten. Even one small slice immediately freezes your entire body. Two slices would turn you into an everlasting ice statue. You'd be so cold you would never melt, even in the searing deserts of Swelter. And if you were able to eat an entire Ice Cucumber . . . well, who knows what might happen!?

Louis nodded and said, 'This is exactly what we need to defeat Borax.'

'If you're going off to look for this koom-bar-bar, then I'm coming too,' said Catalogue. 'I love studying and that, but I loves a good adventure even more.'

Louis was very pleased to hear this. What hero could ask for more than to be joined by a magic sword called Dave, a robot horse called Clunkalot and a smart, friendly boar called Reader Catalogue. What a team!

'So, we knows this thingy grows on the ocean's bottom,' said Catalogue. 'But how is we going to get there? I'm not that good at holding my breath.'

'I'm not sure yet,' said Louis, 'but first let's head to Portly Wishwash!'

'Sounds great,' said Catalogue, 'except I've no idea what a Portly Wishwash is.'

'It's a town,' explained Louis. 'A seaport. I've never been but Mum told me about it. Let's go!'

AHA! SOUNDS LIKE WE'RE HEADING FOR A PIRATE ADVENTURE.

NO. NO YOU'RE THINKING OF THE TOWN OF PORTLY CUTLASS.

YEAH, THIS BOOK'S GOT NOTHING ABOUT PIRATES IN IT.

I SUPPOSE THEY'RE KEEPING THAT FOR ONE OF THE SEQUELS.

KNIGHT SIR LOUIS AND THE PONGY PIRATES?

KNIGHT SIR LOUIS AND THE PUNY PIRATE PRINCE?

KNIGHT SIR LOUIS AND THE PIRATES OF PLOPP?

SHALL WE JUST GET ON WITH THIS STORY?

136

And so, Catalogue locked up her room in Saint Trotter's College and set off with Louis for the town of Portly Wishwash. But not before her graduation ceremony.

Everything went well, except when they went outside to take a photograph. The wind picked up and blew across the blade of Louis' sword, Dave. Dave started to sing, which nobody likes. Well, almost nobody. Walruses love it. A great flumping-galumphing pod of walruses arrived in no time.

'Oh! What lovely music,' said one walrus in walrus language.

'Must be to celebrate this graduation,' said another.

'Everyone say cheese,' said a third.

CHAPTER 21

Well, I don't know about you, but I'm wondering
what Sir Merry-Jingles has been up to.

CHAPTER 22

Knight Sir Merry-Jingles had a simple plan. Follow Louis until he defeated the dragon Borax. Then get rid of Louis and claim the victory for himself.

What a meanie!

Merry-Jingles kept his distance and observed Louis from afar. He had followed Louis to Doooooom and watched the battle with Borax. He had followed Louis on his search for Mysto. And

he had followed him to Hogford. He'd also waited patiently at the library reception for Argie the cyclops.

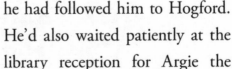

'Oh, hi there!' said Merry-Jingles to Argie with a big friendly smile. 'I bet you've had a long day. Tell me. What was the last book you had to find?'

'I was helping some friends find a book on magical cucumbers,' said Argie.

'What a coincidence,' said Merry-Jingles. 'I'm also looking for that exact book.'

'Phew!' said Argie with a big smile. 'Well, for once, I know exactly where that is!'

Merry-Jingles read about all the different types of cucumber in the book and quickly worked out that the Ice Cucumber must the key to defeating Borax. They'll be heading for the seaside, he thought. This posed a big problem though. Merry-Jingles didn't believe in the sea. Remember Queen Incredulous had always insisted that:

While tracking Louis, Merry-Jingles had already started to wonder about these long-held beliefs. He was pretty sure the Jabby Mountains were not made of rubber. When he'd tracked Louis there, he'd grazed his knee on the rocks.

OUCH!

But maybe it was just really hard rubber? Hmm. Also, when he was in Hogford, he'd visited their Natural History Museum. He'd spent a long time examining the displays on cats and owls. They really did seem to be totally different animals.

Now, he was planning a trip to the seaside. But how could there be a seaside, if there was no sea? It was all very confusing.

On his way out he spotted a very familiar book in the green section.

It was a book by Merry-Jingles' own grand-mother. Despite its name, it was quite a serious book. It was a book about acting. It was required reading for the drama students. Merry-Jingles had his own signed copy from his grandmother. He'd read it at least a dozen times. Here's a little bit:

ACTING GAMES: THE FRIEND GAME

Right then lovelies, in this game, you gotta be the friendliest person you can imagine. When you meet somebody new, try this... try to be their bestest friend ever. Listen to them. Nothing will be too much trouble for you. Make a note of their favourite foods and drinks. Watch for their habits. If they like kick-a-ball, then become a great fan of kick-a-ball too. If they love clambering up mountains, then be a great fan of it too, or an admirer of those that do it. Soon, you'll know loads about them, and be the best of friends.

Merry-Jingles decided it was time for him to put this game to good use. It was time to come out from the shadows. It was time to become Louis' new best friend!

CHAPTER 23

Louis, Clunkalot and Catalogue arrived in Portly Wishwash on a grey day. The sea breeze was cold and couldn't make up its mind about which way to blow, so it blew in all directions at once. The boats in the harbour groaned and creaked as they rocked in the choppy waves. Sailors and merchants and sea passengers walked about here and there. Every single one looked as happy as a John Dory.

'Friendly place,' said Louis, jokingly.

A bunch of burly sailors sat outside an inn called *The Shipwreck* drinking a nasty thick brown ale called Suspicion. As Louis, Clunkie and Catalogue wandered by, they muttered between themselves.

'So, how's we going to get to the ocean's bottom?' asked Catalogue. 'These boats all look pretty floaty to me.'

'We're going to use a submarine,' explained Louis. He wrapped his knuckles on the side of

Clunkalot. 'Or to be more precise, a submarine robot horse. It'll be a bit of a squeeze for both of us, but I'm sure we'll manage.'

'You're sure Clunkie's all waterproof?' asked Catalogue.

'Pretty sure,' said Louis, 'though we've never tested him so deep. I do have dive suits inside, in case of the worst!'

Clunkie neighed and burped out a haiku poem for Catalogue to read.

I WILL KEEP YOU SAFE
BUT REMEMBER ONE SMALL THING
DON'T OPEN THE DOOR
(AT LEAST, NOT WITHOUT YOUR DIVE SUIT)

They climbed inside Clunkie. He raced along the harbourside and launched into the sea. SPLASH!

The sailors outside *The Shipwreck* had watched it all. None of them said anything for a while.

The others groaned and told him it was his turn to buy another round of Suspicion.

CHAPTER 24

Clunkalot dropped down into the harbour waters. He retracted his legs and extended four great flippers. Then his tail started to rotate like a ship's propellor. Very soon, they were out of the murky waters of the harbour and into the open ocean. The further out to sea he went, the deeper the seabed. Clunkalot dived down and turned on his brightest eye-lamps. Inside, Louis and Catalogue watched the screen. They saw many interesting sights as they cruised into the deep sea.

Mum I'm in a submarine!
Seen loads of sharks:
hammerheads, spannerheads,
forkheads! Anyway, still
on mission to stop Borax.
Looking for ice cucumbers.
Have funny feeling
something might go wrong.
Meet me at Castle
Sideways? Say hi to Dad.
      Love Louis

Champion Trixie (AKA MUM)
Chilvary Farm
Squirrel Helm

Hey Argie,
I'm a underwater boar.
Me and Louis have
seen things that'd
make your eye pop out.
Jellyfishes, shrimpees,
fishy-wishes.
I wouldn't mind glowing
like that. Would make
reading at night loads
easier. Anyway,
  see ya. Catalogue xx

Argie Cyclops
Mogford Library
Mogford

152

Things were going smoothly it seemed. Near the surface the sea was bright and beautiful. Deeper down it was mysterious and dark, but nothing a robot horse's headlamps couldn't deal with. At last, they dropped into the very deepest, darkest, coldest part of the ocean where only magical light could reach. That's where things started to go a little bit weird.

Down here the magical light had found itself with very little to do. So, it had played around a bit. Jellyfish had evolved into Jollyfish. Shrimps had evolved into Shrumps. And, as Louis and Catalogue were about to find out, there were more things too.

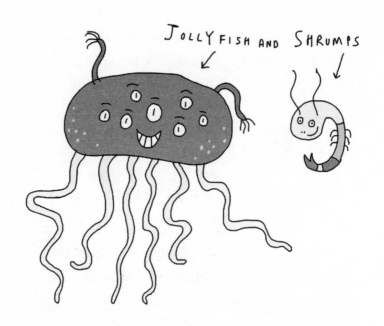

JOLLYFISH AND SHRUMPS

'Er, Louis,' said Catalogue looking at the screen. 'Ever seen a giant rainbow doughnut?'

'No,' said Louis, also looking at the screen. 'Not until now.'

'And, er, Louis,' said Catalogue again. 'Ever seen a giant, rainbow doughnut with a mermaid tail?'

'No,' said Louis. 'Not until now.'

'And one more thing, Louis,' said Catalogue. 'Ever seen a giant, rainbow doughnut with a mermaid's tail and an enormous set of shark's teeth?'

'No,' said Louis, watching as the unbelievable thing came closer and closer. 'Not until now.'

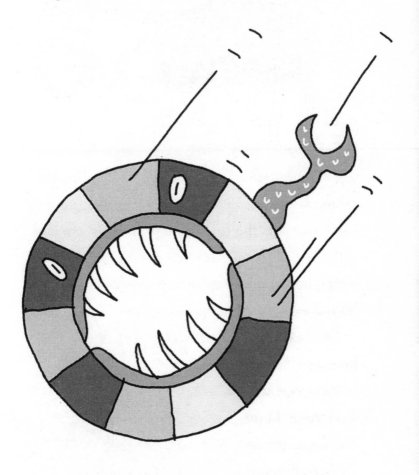

AGHHHHHHH!!!

CHAPTER 25

When Merry-Jingles arrived in Portly Wishwash a few hours after Louis, he found it to be even more miserable. The sun had given up trying to shine through the thick clouds and had gone off early. The unpleasant sea breeze now turned into a whipping wind and was joined by some sideways rain. Nice.

Merry-Jingles rushed for cover. As luck (or unluck) would have it, he rushed into *The Shipwreck* inn. The tough sailors had moved inside. They'd been hoping to play darts, but unfortunately, they'd already thrown the darts in the harbour after a big fight. Now, they took one look at Knight Sir Merry-Jingles and decided they could use him as a dart instead. The only question was, would he stick to the dartboard?

Merry-Jingles sensed he was in trouble, so he decided to put his grandmother's 'Friend Game' to the test straight away.

'How about I buy you all a drink, a hot meal and tell you a few jokes?' said Merry-Jingles.

An hour later, the sailors were transformed into smiling, new friends of Merry-Jingles. None of them could remember when they'd felt so good. The meanest one hadn't just laughed, she'd laughed hardest of them all.

The toast had worried Merry-Jingles. Queen Incredulous had said toast was evil. But when he'd tried a slice, it just seemed to be a tasty kind of burnt bread. Could she be wrong about that too?

The following day Merry-Jingles tried out the Friend Game again on others around the town. He thanked the fishmonger for the (disgusting) fish. He thanked the shirtmaker for the new (very itchy) shirt. He thanked the hotel keeper for the (lumpy) bed. Soon, the people of Portly Wishwash were feeling happier.

They felt appreciated. They started being nicer to each other too. And they started to take more care of what they did. The fishmonger made sure the fish stayed fresh. The shirtmaker selected only the softest fabrics to make new shirts. The hotel keeper ordered some new beds.

Merry-Jingles was amazed to see how well the Friend Game worked. He was alarmed to realise he also felt a warm, fuzzy glow. He felt good about what had happened. He pinched himself. Ow! He didn't want to be nice! He wanted to be EMPEROR!

Now he knew the Friend Game worked, he was ready for Louis. When Louis came back to shore, Merry-Jingles would be waiting. In the meantime, he also wrote a postcard:

My Dearest Love and Queen
Soon, I will claim
victory for us thanks to
an ice cucumber
(Long story)
On a side note, I remember
you saying that 'the sea
does not exist' and 'toast
is evil'. Well, er, it turns
out, er... hmm... oh never
mind. Big smushy kisses!
Mwah mwah. From your
      Merry Jingles

Queen Incredulous
Castle Round the Twist
Klaptrap

Now, before we find out how Louis and Catalogue are getting on with underwater doughnuts, let's just see what's going on with Borax. To start the next chapter . . .

JUST PRESS HERE

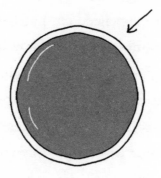

(Or if that doesn't work, just turn to the next page.)

CHAPTER 26

Yargl and Scaba Borax had been busy. They'd laid a whole pile of eggs. Once these eggs hatched out, there would be an army of Boraxes! Yargl and Scaba congratulated themselves on how clever they were. They celebrated by flying to the hill town of Soggy Hoo to set it on fire. Soggy Hoo was famous for being the rainiest place in Squirrel Helm. Yargl and Scaba breathed fire at it all afternoon and then flew home happy that they'd burnt it to the ground. Actually, Soggy Hoo was so wet that all Borax managed to do was create lots and lots of steam. Once it cleared, the town had their first dry, sunny day for a hundred years.

HOORAY!

But then, at around eight o'clock, it started raining again.

BOO! TYPICAL!

Meanwhile, back at Castle Sideways, the courtiers had been busy. They'd let their fears about the dragon run wild. They were saying things like:

None of this was true, but it didn't stop other courtiers from nodding their heads and saying:

These ridiculous rumours quickly spread into the countryside. But then they changed. Some people doubted Borax even existed! People started saying things like:

MY SISTER'S NURSE'S UNCLE KNOWS A PROFESSOR WHO SAYS BORAX IS A GIANT MUSHROOM WITH LASER EYES.

Meanwhile the young wizentor Pearlin had also been busy. She wasn't the sort of person to just sit around waiting for others to save the day all by themselves. And she wasn't the sort of person to listen to rumours and simply believe them. She wanted to know what was REALLY GOING ON!

'What we need, boss,' she told King Burt, 'is more information about this dragon Borax. What makes it tick, you know?'

'What makes it tick?' said King Burt confused. 'Does it tick? Is it some sort of clock? Does it go *BONG* at one o'clock?'

'No,' said Pearlin. 'I mean we need to work out what the dragon does. What it likes. Where it goes. What it eats. The truth!'

And that is why Pearlin invented the Cactusmobile.

While Louis was considering submarines, Pearlin had been thinking about her own special vehicle. The Cactusmobile was designed to look like a big prickly, desert cactus. The sort of thing that would blend in with a desolate landscape.

The Cactusmobile was hollow and inside was a mini laboratory. There was also a bicycle seat and some pedals which powered three tough wheels. You see, Pearlin was going to Dooooooom to keep an eye on Borax. She made sure to take one of her magical emergency keys with her. (She also took a large jelly spoon in case she needed to eat her way out.)

King Burt's guards accompanied Pearlin to the borderlands, pulling the Cactusmobile on a cart behind a dozen horses. Then, they waited for nightfall and Pearlin climbed inside and cycled her big fake plant into the land of dragons. From here on in, she was on her own.

CHAPTER 27

Pearlin cycled her cactus quietly into Doooooom. At first light she felt the ground tremble.

STOMP STOMP STOMP

Something was approaching. She stopped the Cactusmobile and peered out of her peephole. A huge, snake-like yellow dragon with six legs was heading her way. It was time to find out if her hiding place was really hidden! The dragon, known as Cedric the Sulphuric, had woken up because of the delicious smell wafting through the morning air. It smelled like human. One of his favourite snacks.

Cedric was keen to find something quick to eat so he could get back to sitting on his new egg. He didn't remember laying it. In fact, he wasn't sure boy dragons could lay eggs. But there it was. In his nest. A long, reddish egg. Maybe it was magic, or destiny or something? He'd seen that dodgy dragon Borax hanging around. But Borax wouldn't just go around handing out eggs, right?

Cedric followed the smell of human. It was strongest near a cactus. He'd walked this way before, but never noticed this plant. Hmm! He stopped to give it a really good sniff. Pearlin saw the dragon approach. Outside, Cedric was taking in a big snort. Yes. There was the smell of human. Very strong from this cactus! Tasty! And then all of a sudden it changed. He took a really big snort and UGH! The smell of stinking, rotting old cabbage appeared in his nostrils. Cedric felt his stomach turn. He turned and stomped back to his nest, where he coiled up on his egg and spoke gentle words to it.

Pearlin nodded to herself. That had been a close thing! Lucky she had some ready-made stink potion. Phew! She rolled the Cactusmobile onwards into Doooooom.

Back at Castle Sideways, King Burt had watched the whole encounter with Cedric on his TV. It had been nail-biting stuff. King Burt couldn't watch it alone. He'd asked the guards to come in and watch it with him. They'd all been glued to the screen until Cedric turned and wandered off. PHEW!

In fact, as Pearlin's expedition into Doooooom continued, more and more courtiers tuned in to see what she was up to. Very soon, Pearlin's expedition to Dooooooom was being watched by almost everyone in the kingdom. (Including in the outlying regions where TV hadn't been invented yet. They did a puppet show version instead).

Let's tune in ourselves . . .

CHAPTER 28

NARRATOR: And now on Channel One, the only TV programme we have continues. Yes, let's join the wizentor Pearlin as she investigates The Life of Doooooom.

PEARLIN: Picture it. A land scorched by a thousand dragons. A land once covered in lush forest, now a desert of rocks and rubble. But even here, there is life.

PEARLIN: See here, a nest. And inside it, three perfect eggs. The dragon who sits and warms these eggs only ever leaves them for a few minutes. So, we don't have long to admire them.

PEARLIN: See, how these two are round, blue and speckled. These were laid by the dragon. But what about this long, reddish egg? Should that be here?

PEARLIN: No, it's the same sort of egg that I've

seen in nests all over Dooooooom. Just like the cuckoo, one dragon has been laying its eggs in other dragons' nests.

PEARLIN: Most dragons happily sit on these

cuckoo's eggs without question. But at least one has abandoned their nest after finding this strange egg.

PEARLIN: I decided to take the egg for myself.

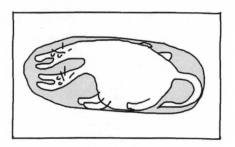

Here's what I've discovered using my wizentor X-ray. That's right . . . this is a bi-dragon egg.

PEARLIN: Right now, I am sat on the egg and

keeping it warm with my own bum. I have to say I've become quite fond of it, even though it's just an egg and even though there's a dangerous animal inside.

PEARLIN: Anyway, I'm hoping for the best. I've

been telling it stories. Telling it I'll look after it and telling it there's no hurry to hatch. It can come out when it feels like it.

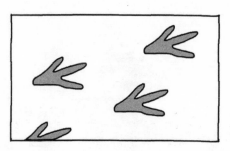

PEARLIN: That's all for now. I've just spotted some large bi-dragon footprints in the dust. I'm going to see if I can find Borax. Wish me luck, and join me again later on THE LIFE OF DOOOOOOM!

CHAPTER 29

Let's get back to Louis and Catalogue now. Do you remember where they were?

AGHHHHHHH!!!

That's right. We left them at AGHHHHHH!!!
Let's see if things are any better now?

AGHHHHHH!!!
No. No better.

Knight Sir Louis and Reader Catalogue were inside Clunkalot and watching the screen. The giant-rainbow-doughnut-mermaid-shark-thing was heading straight for them and chomping its impressive teeth as it came.

Clunkalot lifted a wing and did a spin to his left. The huge beast turned too and came after them. Here are some of the most exciting moments from the chase . . .

179

'We can't keep this up,' said Louis.

'And we's haven't even found the koomumber-bar-bars yet,' said Catalogue.

It was true. Clunkie's headlamp eyeballs weren't very bright down here in the deepest, darkest depths.

'If only we had some way of lighting up the seabed!' Louis said.

And then he clapped himself on the helmet.

'What am I thinking?' he laughed. 'I totally forgot about the gift from Sonya the Shoe Eater! The Light Key!'

(Let's hope you read that chapter!)

Louis had kept the neon-lipped shell gifted to him by Sonya inside Clunkie's storage compartment. He opened the drawer and pulled it out. It was glowing!

'Ooo!' said Catalogue. 'That's a pretty wotsit! What are you going to do with it?'

What Louis did was to pop it into another drawer marked 'recycling' and then pull the lever marked 'empty recycling'.

Moments later Clunkie's tail lifted and the shell popped (or rather plopped) out of his robot bum.

And as soon as the shell touched the sea water, it lit up like a flare. No, brighter than a flare. As bright as an underwater moon! Silver light lit up the sea floor for a mile around.

'WHOA!' said Louis.

And then Catalogue announced . . .

"KOOM BAR BARS!"

Yes! The light key had lit up a whole field of Ice Cucumbers lying right below them.

HOORAY!

But then Louis spotted not one, but two more giant-rainbow-doughnut-mermaid-shark-things hovering over the field.

UNHOORAY!

CHAPTER 30

If there were exams to pass to become a knight, then they might have questions like this . . .

THE KNIGHTLY BOARD OF EXAMINATIONS

KNIGHT OF THE REALM LEVEL 1

STRATEGY PAPER A

Name: Knight Sir Louis
Date: The Year of Our Llama 802

....

You have one hour and thirty minutes to answer the following paper. Marks will be given for style and originality.

....

QUESTION: You are on a mission to collect underwater cucumbers! You are already underwater, riding in your robot horse, but you are suddenly threatened by two giant, hungry fishy monsters. You have with you: a singing sword, a plant expert and a robot horse. How do you complete your mission and survive?

Answer: It makes sense for the group to split into two teams. Can't write any more as I'm doing this RIGHT NOW!

CHAPTER 31

It was time for Louis and Catalogue to get swimming! They put on their dive suits. Catalogue swam down amongst the Ice Cucumber plants. The plants rambled all over the sea floor. She set about collecting as many as she could handle.

Meanwhile, Louis, Clunkalot and Dave got busy distracting the giant-rainbow-doughnut-mermaid-shark-things. Dave usually started singing when a strong wind blew across his sharp edge. But, of course, underwater there was no wind. Louis opened the hatch on Clunkalot's side. He swung up to sit on Clunkie's back.

'Let's see if this works,' said Louis hopefully and Clunkie started paddling faster. Then Louis unsheathed Dave the sword and held him up high. The blade sliced through the water.

'Faster, Clunkie!' said Louis.

Clunkie spun his tail faster than he'd even done before. He wasn't sure he could keep it up for long, but he didn't need to. He just had to get Dave to start singing.

Soon the water was passing over Dave's sharp edge and Dave started to sing. It didn't sound the same as in the air. In the air Dave sounded sort of high-pitched.

EEeeeEEEkEEeekkkkeeEEEEEeeek

But underwater he sounded lower . . .

Urrrrrrggggle Burrrrrbleeee Flurrrrrgllllle

It still sounded horrible though. And as luck would have it, it was still exactly the sort of music that walruses liked.

In hardly any time at all a herd of walruses were swimming down to listen to the vile music.

IS THIS A WONDERFUL NEW SONG FROM DAVE?

IT'S A WATERY MASTERPIECE.

HIS BEST YET.

Very soon there were hundreds of walruses swimming around. This really confused the giant-rainbow-doughnut-mermaid-shark-things. They looked around at the walruses and noticed their big tusks. It didn't seem very sensible to stick around. Something deep down inside their little sharky brains said, 'Teeth and tusks aren't a fun combination if you're made of doughnuts.'

And so they turned and swam off into the darkness.

'It worked!' said Louis and once he was sure they were gone, he put his sword away.

The walruses were not impressed.

Louis and Clunkie dived down towards the cucumbers just as Catalogue swam up out of the tangle of plants. She was holding a bunch of about twelve.

'Well done, Catalogue,' said Louis. 'Now, let's

get back to dry land. It's time to head home. We've got a dragon that needs chilling out.'

So, there we go. At last, Knight Sir Louis has the fabled Ice Cucumbers he needs to defeat the terrible Borax!

SURELY, NOTHING CAN GO WRONG NOW.

AW! WHY DID YOU HAVE TO SAY THAT?!

SOMETHING'S BOUND TO GO WRONG NOW.

CHAPTER 32

Back in Dooooooom, Pearlin had found one of Borax's caves on the side of a low mountain. It didn't look like much from the outside, but inside was a different matter. Let's tune back into Pearlin's TV show and see what's going on . . .

PEARLIN: Hi, it's Pearlin here. I've found Yargl and Scaba Borax's cave! They're out right now, so let's go in and see what's what!

PEARLIN: Okay, I'm taking the Cactusmobile in now.

PEARLIN: So, it's well dark in here except for one shaft of light. There are some big candles here. I'm lighting one. Whoa! Look at this!

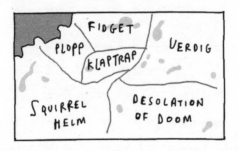

PEARLIN: Borax has scratched a map of the Many Kingdoms onto the walls. And here is a plan of action. It reads . . .

Fly around and destroy everything until everything is destroyed.
Ha Ha Ha Ha!
Starting with Castle Sideways

Oh no!

PEARLIN: Agh. I can hear a cracking sound.

PEARLIN: What's that? Oh! It's the egg I've been sitting on. It's hatching, here and now! I hope it doesn't want to eat me! Hello, little one. Recognise my voice? I've been keeping you warm. Yeah? Don't chew my head off? What do you say?

BABY DRAGON: *Mama!*

PEARLIN: Aw! Phew! I thought I was in trouble then. Better give you a name I suppose. What about . . . Mac n Cheese? Sorry, but, you know, I'm feeling a bit hungry.

MAC N CHEESE: *Coooooo!*

PEARLIN: Hey what's that other noise? Not like a crack. More like a rumble, rumble, boom. Uh-oh! I think I am in trouble. Borax is home. Wish me luck, everyone!

CHAPTER 33

It was early morning in Portly Wishwash. The sun was shining. The people of the town were smiling. Thanks to Merry-Jingles and his Friend Game, the town had transformed from a mean, hard port town into a sort of jolly holiday resort.

The sailors sat on the quayside smiling.

Also sitting with them was their new best friend, Knight Sir Merry-Jingles. He was watching the sea and waiting. Then, all of a sudden, something leapt out of the water and landed in front of them. It was Clunkalot. The hatch opened and a pile of Ice Cucumbers rolled out, with Louis and Catalogue stepping out afterwards.

'Hooray, we did it!'

The friends laughed and hugged.

Knight Sir Merry-Jingles smiled a sly smile. It was time to become Louis' new best friend. He leapt up.

'I say! Another knight! Lovely to meet you! Sir Merry-Jingles is the name. Is there anything I can do to help?'

Louis turned to him, surprised by the welcome.

Merry-Jingles smiled a big smile. The biggest he could manage. It was so wide his cheeks bulged like boxing gloves.

But something inside Louis' brain said, 'Hey. That's weird. Look at his eyes. His mouth is smiling. But his eyes aren't. His eyes are saying, I'm gonna get you, ha ha ha ha!'

'I wonder. Can I help you with your cucumbers?' asked Merry-Jingles. 'I'm sure my friends and I can help you find a box or something?'

Louis was ready to refuse the offer, but Catalogue spoke first.

'Oo!' said Catalogue. 'That'd be nice. Cheers!'

Soon, Merry-Jingles and his sailor friends had found a lovely box for the cucumbers. They'd even found a nice lid. And a ribbon to tie it with. With a bow! Louis had to agree, they'd done a lovely job.

When it was ready Merry-Jingles said, 'You both look exhausted. Let me make you a meal before you go on your way.'

Even Louis couldn't argue with that. He was starving. Merry-Jingles led them to *The Shipwreck* and found them a table in a quiet corner. Very soon the smell of delicious grilled fish wafted over to them. Ahhhhh! Louis and Catalogue couldn't wait to eat.

Merry-Jingles came over with two plates stuffed with fish, buttery potatoes and a salad.

'Eat it up!' he said with another one of his face-stretching smiles.

Louis and Catalogue tucked in.

Nom nom nom!

Now, let's take a closer look at this meal.

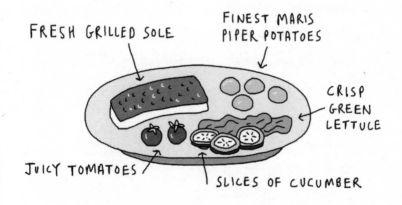

FRESH GRILLED SOLE

FINEST MARIS PIPER POTATOES

CRISP GREEN LETTUCE

JUICY TOMATOES

SLICES OF CUCUMBER

HANG ON!
SLICES OF ICE CUCUMBER?!
OH NO!

Yes. While Merry-Jingles had been boxing up the cucumbers, he'd slipped one inside his armour. Then he'd chopped it up and served it to Louis and Catalogue. His latest plan was simple and cunning.

Oh! Flibberty Jibberty Nan!
Oh! Jingerly Jangerly Jor!
Here's my simply amazing plan,
to freeze the knight and the boar!

I'll give them a salad to eat,
with cucumber, evenly sliced,
and after they've gobbled their treat
they'll be nicely, freshly iced!

Then off I'll go to Doooooom,
with the leftover veg in a box.
I'll find that dragon and BOOM!
When it eats up the veg: what shocks!

Then who'll be the hero on high,
when the dragon is cold as stone?
Me, I'm the one, I'm the guy!
All the world will be my own!

It had worked too! They were wolfing down the food as fast as they could. Ha ha! Knight Sir Merry-Jingles didn't waste any time. He ran out of the inn, grabbed the box of Ice Cucumbers, jumped onto his hobby horse and galloped (sort of) out of town.

FASTER FASTER!

CHAPTER 34

Louis wolfed down his food. He wasn't normally a wolfer. Growing up, his farmer dad was always telling him to eat more slowly.

'It took time to grow, son,' he'd say. 'So, take time to eat it.'

But right now, Louis was starving. He wolfed down the fish. He wolfed down the potatoes. And he wolfed down the salad, including a slice of Ice Cucumber. Beside him Catalogue was snaffling down her meal too. She was usually a snaffler because she'd spent her early life competing for her food with eight brothers and sisters.

Then suddenly!

CRACKKKK!

Louis shivered, then turned blue, then . . . froze solid!

MARTHA THIS BOOK
SHOULD'VE BEEN
CALLED KNIGHT SIR
MERRY-JINGLES AND
THE DRAGON OF DOOOOOOM?

Catalogue looked at Louis, shocked. Then she looked down at her plate. She had snaffled down the fish. She had snaffled down the potatoes. And she had snaffled down her salad too. Well, almost all of it. She'd left the one vegetable she wasn't that keen on.

Cucumbers.

She leant in and looked at the slices carefully.

There was ice forming at their edges.

'Oh bunglers,' said Catalogue, 'these is Ice Koombarbars! That Merry-Jingles ain't as friendly on the insides as he is on the outsides.'

Catalogue tried everything to warm Louis up. She tried pouring a hot cup of coffee between his lips. But the coffee froze solid as soon as it touched his mouth. She tried running him a hot bath. The sailors helped to lift Louis in. It had no effect. Finally, she remembered Clunkalot had a hair-dryer function. She ran out onto the quayside, carrying the frozen Louis. Clunkie breathed hot air over Louis, on his highest super-hot setting. But that didn't work either.

Catalogue was worried and out of ideas.

'Aw! Clunkie,' she said to the robot horse, 'what are we gonna do?'

Clunkalot was upset too. He couldn't even think of a good poem.

As they stood there despairing, a boat moored up and started to unload its cargo. A merchant strolled over to the captain of the boat.

'Excuse me, are those chilli peppers? How much for ten boxes?'

Catalogue turned her head. Chilli peppers! Maybe that might work?

'I'll have a box and all,' she said, rushing over.

The peppers were long and thin and red. She crushed up the whole box with her trotters, filled up a tall glass with red, hot juice and poured it onto Louis' lips. And guess what?

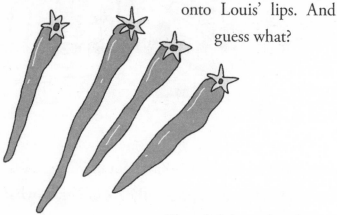

That didn't work either.

But it did give Reader Catalogue (expert in plants with an advanced degree in Weird Botany) an idea.

CHAPTER 35

Back in Dooooooom, Pearlin was stuck inside her Cactusmobile as Borax returned home to the cave. Yargl and Scaba Borax weren't stupid. They knew they didn't have a cactus growing inside their cave. Luckily, Pearlin had planned for this moment. Just before Borax came back she flicked a large piece of paper out of the spy hatch. When Borax came home the first thing they noticed was the cactus. They were about to obliterate it with a fireball, when they spotted the paper and read:

To Borax,
a small present from an admirer.
We hope you enjoy your dragon slaying,
big - bang - Boom exploding cactus.

Simply set fire to it, or touch it, or sniff it and it will blow you to smithereens. Good riddance!

Borax chuckled to themselves.

'Ha, ha!' they said. 'Can't fool us. We'll just leave this cactus here. If we don't touch it, it won't explode. HA!'

'Phew!' said the cactus. 'Glad that worked.'

Yargl and Scaba Borax had returned to the cave because they knew their eggs were starting to hatch. And that meant it was time to hatch their plans too.

Left to their own devices, the little baby bi-dragons might settle down in their new homes and grow up to be perfectly nice beasts. But while they were still so little, they could be hypnotised by Borax's homing call. This was a special dragon song that attracted their babies and called them all together.

I know what you're thinking. You're thinking it was something silly like:

OOODALEEBOODALEHOOOO!
OOODALEEBOODALEHOOOO!

But, actually, it was more like:

The low song echoed all around Dooooooom. And very soon there was a trail of tiny bi-dragons heading for Borax's cave. They filed in until the place was full of them.

Pearlin couldn't hear anything. But she could see Scaba and Yargl opening and shutting their mouths for some reason. And she could see something was having a strange effect on Mac n Cheese. They were nodding their heads strangely. Pearlin checked her instruments and realised Borax was singing so low that it was impossible to hear. She tried covering up Mac n Cheese's ears with a duvet, some cushions and a towel. She hoped it would be enough to stop them falling under Borax's hynoptic spell.

Borax's song stopped and Pearlin checked under the duvet to see if Mac n Cheese were okay.

They weren't there.

OH NO!

Pearlin peered out from her Cactusmobile and saw Mac n Cheese, with glazed, hypnotised eyes, joining her siblings. Pearlin's mind raced. She had to find a way to get little Mac n Cheese back. She suddenly realised how much she cared for the little beast. She undid the hatch on the side of the Cactusmobile and reached out. She caught Mac n Cheese by the tail.

'And now,' said Yargl and Scaba with one voice, 'it is time for chaos. WE FLY!'

Pearlin tried to pull Mac n Cheese back towards her. But they turned around with mouths open and fangs bared. They snapped at Pearlin. Mac got a little bite in and Pearlin cried out. 'AGH!'

The cave was suddenly very silent. All the little bi-dragons turned to look at Pearlin. Borax looked too.

'A-ha. I see!' said Yargl. 'You tricked us! Clever.'

'Yes, we must fly. But first,' said Scaba, 'there's time for a little snack of roasted wizard!'

Borax took a deep breath and prepared to blast out a bolt of dragon fire. And quick as a flash, Pearlin climbed back inside the Cactusmobile and turned her emergency key.

BLOOP!

CHAPTER 36

Reader Catalogue was back in Hogford. Clunkalot was parked up outside the library.

Poor, frozen Louis was inside Clunkie's belly, still as solid and as cold as an iceberg on a skiing holiday.

Catalogue went straight to Argie the cyclops at the library.

'I needs a book on chillies and peppers and stuff,' explained Catalogue.

'I know just the book you need. But it's out at the moment. The Professor of Dangerous Cocktails is using it. And I wouldn't try and get it off him!' said Argie.

'But I needs to know what the hottest vegetable is ever in the history of history! And I needs it urgent!'

'Let's try the archives!' said Argie, and they raced off.

The archives were in the basement, deep under the library. Corridor after corridor of cupboards, boxes and drawers. This was where the university stored all the interesting things that its explorers and scientists had found down through the ages.

They included . . .

The Bog Meteorite

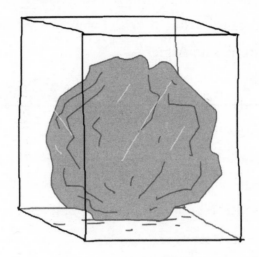

Smashed into the Bogs of Wattasmel after falling from space. Sent up a huge wave of stinking mud that covered the local villages. They had to be abandoned forever as the smell couldn't be washed away. The meteorite was retrieved with magic. Now stored in a smell-proof case.

Dinodrackon Footprint

A fossilised footprint of a prehistoric dragon! Much bigger than today's living dragons, the Dinodrackon flattened anything it stood on.

Tractorina's Trotter Shoes

Legend has it these are the shoes belonging to the original founder of Hogford University. They look a bit like time-travelling shoes, if you ask me.

Argie took Catalogue to a low, wooden set of drawers.

'This is it!' he said. 'Now be very careful. These things are seriously hot.'

He slid open a drawer and inside were some very dry, very wrinkly, very red chilli peppers.

'These have been down here for fifty years,' he explained, 'ever since they were collected from inside the crater of Mount Badaboom.'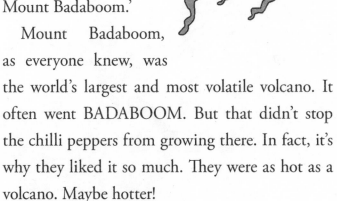

Mount Badaboom, as everyone knew, was the world's largest and most volatile volcano. It often went BADABOOM. But that didn't stop the chilli peppers from growing there. In fact, it's why they liked it so much. They were as hot as a volcano. Maybe hotter!

'If anything can unfreeze your friend, it's one of these,' said Argie.

'But what if they is so hot he turns into a melted marshmallow?' said Catalogue, worried.

'Oh yes,' said Argie worriedly, and he started to push the drawer shut again.

Catalogue stopped him.

'There's no choice,' said Catalogue. 'I have to give it a goes.'

Argie fetched some thick gloves and a pair of tongs. Very carefully, Catalogue picked up the very smallest chilli.

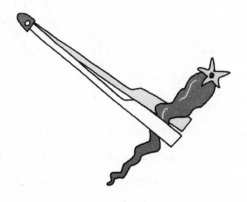

CHAPTER 37

Knight Sir Merry-Jingles should have been feeling very happy with himself. He had the Ice Cucumbers strapped to a box on his back. He had outwitted the world's so-called 'best knight'. All he had to do now was feed a cucumber to a dragon. And how hard could that be?! Weren't they always eating things? Then the world would be his (and Queen Incredulous' too, of course).

However, on his journey home, galloping along on Hobson the hobby horse, he wasn't feeling happy at all. He had a nasty feeling in his stomach every time he thought about Knight Sir Louis and Catalogue. Giving them the Ice Cucumbers to eat was such a nasty thing to do. He didn't feel good about it. At all.

And he couldn't help thinking about the great times he'd had in Portly Wishwash.

I MISS THE SEA AIR
I MISS THE FRIENDSHIP OF THE TOWNSFOLK AND THE SAILORS.
I EVEN MISS THE CONSTANT CALLS OF THE SEABIRDS.
MOST OF ALL, I MISS PEOPLE LIKING ME!
I SHOULD PUT IT ALL BEHIND ME.
I'M GOING TO BE AN EMPEROR!
THAT WILL BE EVEN MORE FUN.
RIGHT? RIGHT?

ESPECIALLY WITH MY ONE TRUE LOVE QUEEN INCREDULOUS. WHO BELIEVES TOAST IS EVIL. AND THAT OWLS ARE CATS WITH WINGS. THAT 34 IS THE BIGGEST NUMBER IN THE UNIVERSE. WHO TELLS ME THE SEA ISN'T REALLY THERE. THAT MOUNTAINS ARE MADE OF RUBBER. OH DEAR! I MUST PUT THESE WORRIES OUT OF MY MIND! I MUST GET TO DOOOOOOOM! AND FIND BORAX.

You may be thinking that Knight Sir Merry-Jingles seems different somehow, perhaps almost a little brave. He is, after all, prepared to go to Doooooom and find the dragon Borax. And in a way, it's true. Merry-Jingles would never have dared to do this in his old days as a jester in the kingdom of Klaptrap. But since then, he's travelled far and wide. He's discovered that he can look after himself quite well.

But, as it turned out, he didn't need to travel all the way to Doooooom to meet the dragon. He found himself passing close to Castle Sideways and decided to take a look. He'd never seen the place. He wondered if it was all that special. He always wondered how it compared to his own home at Castle Round-the-Twist. As he approached the strangest thing happened . . . a giant cube of jelly appeared in front of the castle hill and wobbled. There appeared to be a cactus stuck inside the jelly. Weird!

He turned his hobby horse and rode closer. As he came near, someone emerged from inside. It was a young wizentor with a spoon. She had a mouthful of jelly.

'Wotcha, I'm Pearlin!' she said.

She had escaped from Borax's cave using her emergency key, and just like Louis, had appeared surrounded by jelly. This time, lemon flavour.

'Tell me, where am I?' she asked Merry-Jingles.

'Castle Sideways I think,' he replied.

'Nice one,' she said, then asked, 'you a knight?'

'Errrrrrr . . . yes?'

'Good, we're gonna need you. There are like five hundred dragons coming this way. And they've all got two heads. So that makes a thousand fire-breathers!'

Suddenly, Merry-Jingles' heart sank. It sounded like one box of Ice Cucumbers wasn't going to be much use after all.

CHAPTER 38

YES, YES, YES!

BUT WHAT ABOUT LOUIS AND THE CHILLI?

Okay, okay!

CHAPTER 39

At Castle Sideways, Pearlin explained the dragon situation to King Burt the Not Bad. He immediately ordered everyone into the cave under the mountain for safety.

Then he held an emergency meeting in the great hall. Sitting at the banqueting table were King Burt himself, Pearlin, Knight Sir Merry-Jingles and Louis' mother, Champion Trixie. She'd received her postcard from Louis and had arrived to help just the day before.

'Pearlin tells me we have perhaps one hour before Borax and their little dragons are here,' explained the king. 'So, the big question is, what are we going to have for pudding after dinner?'

228

'I don't think that is the big question, your majesty,' said Pearlin.

'Hmm. You're right. I think the big question is actually, how are we going to stop Borax from burning down this castle and wiping out the entire kingdom?'

King Burt had more reason than anyone to dislike Borax. Borax had eaten his brother Garibaldi (who had smelled faintly of biscuits).

'Let's have some ideas,' said the king.

'We could make a life-size inflatable mountain and castle,' suggested Pearlin. 'Then Borax might attack that instead of the real place.'

'Knowing Borax,' said Trixie, 'he'd burn that down, then find the real one and burn it down too. No, we need a way to stop Borax for good.'

'Er, excuse me, I've got an idea,' said Merry-Jingles putting his hand up, 'we could use . . . Ice Cucumbers.' He put the box on the table. 'And I just happen to have a few here.'

Champion Trixie eyed them suspiciously. 'Ice cucumbers? And how did you come by these?'

'Err . . . I bought them from a . . . er . . . a person,' he lied.

'Really,' said Trixie. 'What person?'

'Err . . . a person with err . . . eyes and hair and a nose and stuff,' said Merry-Jingles.

Champion Trixie's visor was down, but somehow, he still felt her eyes boring into him.

'Where?' she asked.

'Portly Wishwash,' he said without thinking.

'I see,' she said.

An instant later she had leapt across the table, kicked Merry-Jingles' chair backwards to the ground, and had her sword at his chest.

'What have you done with my son?' she barked.

'Right here, Mum!' said a voice and everyone looked up.

It was Louis, with Catalogue and Clunkie.

He was back!

CHAPTER 40

~AND NOW~
THE VERY QUICK CONFESSION
OF
KNIGHT SIR MERRY-JINGLES

I did it! I did it all! I'm sorry!

Signed
Maxwell Merry-Jingles

P.S. I am actually very sorry I thought I wanted to be emperor but actually don't anymore and all I want is to go back to Portly Wishwash where people like me and even think my jokes are funny please don't lock me in the dungeons I'll help defeat Borax just tell me how I can help.

CHAPTER 41

Louis gave his mum a massive and very metallic hug.

CLANG! BONG!

Then Louis and Catalogue joined the others at the table for the emergency meeting.

'These Ice Cucumbers are the key to victory,' explained Louis.

'The trick is getting Borax to eat one,' said Champion Trixie.

'Before they is setting a-fire to the nice old castle,' said Catalogue.

'But what about the rest of the dragons?' said Merry-Jingles.

'I've got another idea. Maybe even better than my inflatable castle one. If we take Borax out, maybe their hypnotic effect on the others will stop,' said Pearlin. 'I really hope so.'

She was thinking about poor Mac n Cheese. The last thing she wanted to do was freeze Mac n Cheese forever!

They cracked open the box with the Ice Cucumbers.

'Oh nos,' said Catalogue looking at the mushy mess inside. 'Most of them's gone all whiffy-rotten.'

She looked up at Merry-Jingles accusingly. 'Didn't you repack them in ice and stuff?'

'Afraid not,' said Merry-Jingles, feeling like a right bungler.

Catalogue looked through the mess of rotting vegetables and retrieved three that were still good.

'Three will have to do,' said Louis. 'Let's hope it's enough.'

Just then, they heard the Klaxongoyle.

'OI! YOU LOT! THERE'S SOMEFING COMING! WATCH OUT! OI! YOU LISTENIN TO ME? WAKE UP YOU LAZY BUNCH! COR BLIMEY!'

They ran over to the balcony. The sky to the west was turning red. But it wasn't the sunset.

It was Borax and their five hundred bi-dragons.

CHAPTER 42

AND SO, IT BEGINS...

WHO'S GOT
THE POPCORN?

HERE IT IS!

IS IT SALTY
OR SWEET?

IT'S PARMESAN
CHEESE FLAVOUR
WITH TRUFFLE
SHAVINGS.

— FANCY!

Knight Sir Louis sat on his trusty steed Clunkalot and raced through the skies. Meanwhile,
Reader Catalogue was inside Clunkalot looking

after the delicate Ice Cucumbers. She was ready to load them into Clunkie's firing mechanism.

Back at the castle, Pearlin was running to the big cube of lemon jelly where her Cactusmobile was stuck. She handed out some spoons to the castle guards and told them to get eating! She needed her Cactusmobile back as soon as possible. She'd had an idea of how to break Borax's hypnotic spell.

Champion Trixie made it her business to look after King Burt and make sure he didn't get gobbled up like his brother. They went to the caves under the castle and Merry-Jingles came with them. The castle folk were huddled together and looking very unhappy. Champion Trixie looked across at Merry-Jingles.

'Your first occupation was as a jester, correct?' she asked.

'Yes,' said Merry-Jingles, 'but Queen Incredulous never found me very funny.'

'Well, now's your chance to try again,' she said.

'Everyone down here is pretty scared. So, why don't you try and cheer them up?'

Merry-Jingles looked at the crowd of people. It was a good-sized audience. It was worth a try!

CHAPTER 43

 AND SO, THE BATTLE...

Borax was flying fast towards the castle. Here it was. The first target in a whole new campaign of chaos! But just then, Yargl and Scaba saw something. Flying up from the castle and coming towards them. Just like that irritating little thing that came after them in Dooooooom before. They'd burned that to a crisp, surely? It couldn't be the same thing, could it?

Yes it could!

Clunkalot approached Borax fast.

'We're not going to have many chances to get this right,' Knight Sir Louis shouted to Clunkie and Catalogue. 'I'll get close and when Borax opens their mouths to breathe fire . . . that's our moment.'

But as he came closer, Borax called out to the other bi-dragons. They rearranged themselves around Borax, creating a shield of other, much smaller dragons.

'We're going to have to fly through them,' Louis said to Clunkie.

Clunkie printed him out a poem.

Measure your desire
by asking how much woe
you are prepared to take

NOT ONE OF HIS FUNNY ONES THEN ?

They raced towards the bi-dragons, desperately hoping to barge through. Louis raised his magical sword Dave. The young dragons could only manage little fire balls and Dave had no problem eating them up and spitting them back out. Soon, Louis was through, and there was Borax!

'Prepare to meet your doom, dragon of Doooooom!' shouted Louis.

'Not our doom!' laughed Yargl. 'We, Borax, Doooooom dragon of Doooooom, will be your doomful doom on this doomful day of doom. Ha ha ha!'

'DOOOOOOOOOOOOOM!' shouted Scaba just for the fun of it.

'Oh whatever,' said Louis. 'GET READY, CATALOGUE!'

Yargl opened his mouth to breathe fire.

Louis straightened Clunkie and pulled them into the firing line.

'NOW!' shouted Louis.

Catalogue popped an Ice Cucumber into Clunkie's firing mechanism and pulled the trigger.

'KOOMBARBAR AWAY!' she shouted.

PLOCK!

At the very last moment, a flight of the young bi-dragons threw themselves in front of Yargl. And BOINK the cucumber bounced off one of them and fell to the earth below.

'MISSED!' shouted Louis. And he pulled Clunkie hard to one side.

Yargl and Scaba prepared to scorch Louis.

The young bi-dragons cleared a path and Borax burst out a series of huge fire bolts! Clunkie did some really smart flying and just avoided being turned into a molten pile of junk.

'We need to get rid of these little dragons,' said Louis urgently. 'But how?'

Fortunately, Pearlin had been up to something.

CHAPTER 44

Pearlin's Cactusmobile had been freed from its citrus jelly prison by the gobbling guards. Now, she was back inside and checking her instruments.

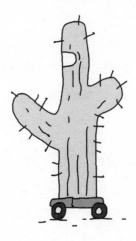

Yes! There it was. The recording of Borax's hynoptic song. The song that went . . .

Pearlin turned her transmitter towards the five hundred little dragons. Then she said a few magic words to reverse the hypnotic song. Then she played it as loud as she could.

High up in the air, Mac n Cheese were feeling strange. Just a moment ago, they'd been feeling very angry.

They'd wanted to protect the big dragon called Borax. They'd have done anything for Borax. But now, suddenly, Mac n Cheese felt different. It was like a fog clearing from their minds. Mac n Cheese suddenly wondered what had happened to their Mummy Pearlin? They missed her a lot!

All around Mac n Cheese, something similar was happening. The reverse song was working. All the little bi-dragons were remembering who they really were. And they were really missing all their adoptive parents. Instead of flying in formation, they were suddenly flapping around in confusion. Most of them turned around and headed back for the land of Doooooom.

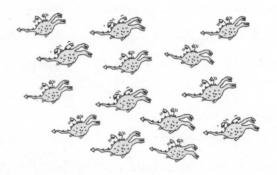

Yargl and Scaba saw them turning away. They could hear the strange anti-hypnotic call in the air, too. Who was making it? How? They became even more angry than normal, which was really, very angry.

It also made them more determined than ever to incinerate Castle Sideways.

CHAPTER 45

Louis and Clunkalot watched as the little dragons turned tail and headed home.

'I don't know what just happened,' said Louis, 'but I'll bet it's Pearlin's doing. What a wizentor she is!' Once more, they flew straight towards Borax.

Borax wasn't far from the castle now.

Yargl and Scaba prepared to do their worst. Yargl opened his mouth first. Louis lined up Clunkalot.

'NOW!' he shouted to Catalogue.

'KOOMBARBAR AWAY!' called Catalogue and the second Ice Cucumber shot out of Clunkie's mouth.

It shot through the sky towards Yargl's mouth, leaving a trail of ice crystals behind it.

A moment before Yargl breathed out a fire bolt, the Ice Cucumber hit home.

It slid into his mouth, down his long neck and into his belly. There was an almighty belch of steam and smoke as the dragon's fire was put out.

But Yargl and Scaba were still very much unfrozen.

'Pesky knight!' shouted Scaba. 'We may not have fire! But we have teeth and claws!'

Borax flew towards Louis, and Clunkalot turned and flipped and loop-the-looped. But it wasn't enough. Borax was fast and strong and lashed out with their long tail. It whipped into Clunkalot and he was sent spinning down, down, down.

Clunkie crashed into the ground outside the cave under the castle hill. His side hatch slammed

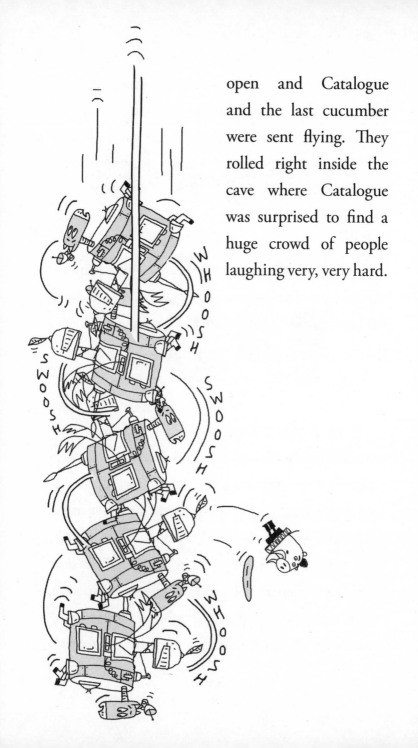

open and Catalogue and the last cucumber were sent flying. They rolled right inside the cave where Catalogue was surprised to find a huge crowd of people laughing very, very hard.

CHAPTER 46

Knight Sir Merry-Jingles had been keeping people's spirits up with his jokes and pratfalls. King Burt thought the jester especially funny. Just as Merry-Jingles was about to do an encore, Catalogue came rolling inside the cave, followed closely by an Ice Cucumber.

'Louis needs a-help,' shouted Catalogue. 'We got one koombarbar inside the nasty old dragon, but it's still going!'

Louis' mum Trixie picked up the cucumber and raced out.

'I'm on it!' she said.

Outside, Clunkie was picking himself up. One of his wings was damaged. He wasn't going to be able to fly again until he'd had some repairs. But where was Louis? Trixie saw him off to her right. Louis stood on a small mound of earth with his sword Dave raised above him. Then she saw Borax racing down from the sky to her left. There wasn't much time!

'POPPET!' she shouted, because that's what she called Louis.

He
turned and
saw his mum hurl
something towards him as
hard as she could.

He looked up at it as it arced
down. Of course! It was the last
Ice Cucumber. This was it.

The last chance.

Borax was bearing down on him, mouths open, fangs exposed, ready to snap him down. Louis turned Dave to his flat, non-sharp side and swung him like a bat.

THWACK!

The Ice Cucumber hit the flat of the blade and was sent soaring towards Scaba's mouth.

The magical vegetable disappeared inside.

There was an almighty CRACCKKKK-CKKCKCKK!

And suddenly Borax was no longer red . . .

. . . but blue and icy!

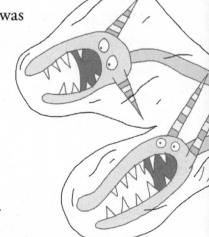

Borax landed hard on the earth and slipped towards Louis. He dived out of the way as the dragon slid, and slid, and slid . . . and then stopped.

They'd done it! They'd stopped Borax!

HOORAY!

BORAX IS FROZEN FROM TOP TO TAIL.

YEAH RIGHT.

Not right.

No.

Not completely.

Borax's bottom half and tail were still red. Louis looked at it and remembered . . . Pearlin's X-ray. The other brain! The brain in the tail!

CHAPTER 47

Yargl and Scaba were frozen. Gone forever. Their brains had been cunning and masterful. But there had always been a third voice inside the dragon. This one was from the smaller brain in the dragon's tail. It called itself Btm. It had never had much to do. It was really only good at moving the tail around, and usually that was just doing what it was told by Yargl and Scaba. At last, the others had shut up!

'Must mean I'm in charge now,' said Btm.

Unbelievably, Btm was even more nasty than Yargl and Scaba. Btm couldn't wait to start burning, chomping and destroying. It was going to be a lot of fun, starting with that stupid knight out there. Btm realised the first thing it needed to do was get the dragon fire going again. Btm did some thinking and found all the bits inside Borax's tummy that made things hot. It started them going. As hot as they could go. All at once. Unfortunately, Btm had no idea what it was doing and three seconds later . . .

The one remaining brain of feared bi-dragon Borax of DOOOOOOM! thought,

'OOOOOOH NOOOOOO!' and then . . .

CHAPTER 48

Louis was getting ready for another battle with Borax's red tail when all of a sudden, the dragon just exploded.

Suddenly there was a roar! But it wasn't a dragon.

It was King Burt, Merry-Jingles and the people of Castle Sideways. They rushed out onto the plain to celebrate their heroes: Trixie, Clunkie, Catalogue, Pearlin and, of course, Knight Sir Louis!

FINAL SCORE

TEAM LOUIS **1 0** TEAM BORAX

CHAPTER
LOOSE ENDS

Hurray! Another victory for Louis and his friends.

PHEW! I THOUGHT THIS BOOK WAS GOING TO HAVE A TRAGIC ENDING FOR A MOMENT.

WHAT REALLY?

NAH. NOT REALLY.

Let's just tidy up a few loose ends, shall we?

Knight Sir Merry-Jingles

 Merry-Jingles returned to Castle Round-the-Twist. He explained to the queen about toast and cats and the sea and all that, hoping she'd come round. Would she like to move with him to the seaside? No, she told him, she would not like that at all, and demanded he cut off his own head. Luckily for him, Knight Sir Daisy broke out of the castle prisons with the help of the other inmates. They took over the kingdom and now Knight Sir Daisy is President Daisy of The Klaptrap Republic. The whereabouts of Queen Incredulous are unknown. Merry-Jingles moved to Portly Wishwash where he is their champion knight and also chief entertainer.

Mac n Cheese

Mac n Cheese flew back to Doooooom

to look for Pearlin, but of course she wasn't there. Fortunately, Pearlin did a quick fix on Clunkalot's bent wing and flew there with Louis. They found Mac n Cheese and brought them home. The bi-dragon now lives with Pearlin at Castle Sideways. Someday, they'll be too big to live in her laboratory, but for now, they are cute and small and also double up as the central heating.

The four hundred and ninety-nine other bi-dragons

The other bi-dragons returned to their adopted parents where they are being looked after very nicely, thank you very much.

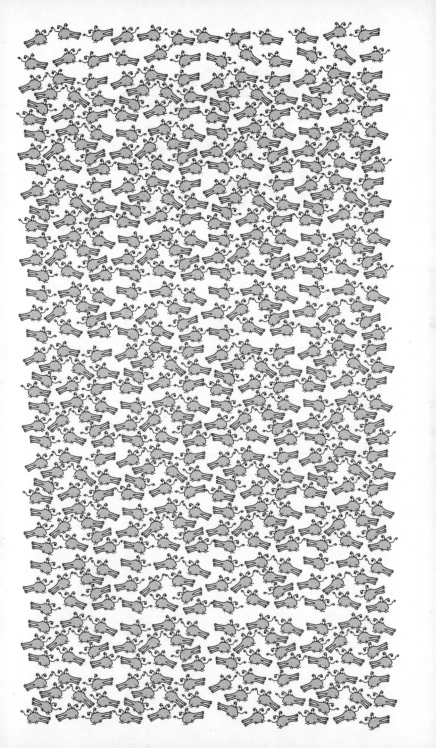

CHAPTER
EVEN MORE
LOOSE ENDS

You might be wondering what happened to Mysto the wizentor (if you read Chapter 15)? We never did work out where he'd gone! Well, remember those rocks in the Jabby Mountains? The ones that make you forget?

After all the excitement of Borax, Louis remembered being there and remembered not remembering (if you see what I mean). He returned and with the help of a spell of Pearlin's they managed to clear the rocks. Inside

WHO AM I? WHO ARE YOU? WHAT IS WHO? WHO IS WHAT? FRIBBLE. SWUOOB.

they found a dwarf with absolutely no idea who he was . . .

It was Mysto. And once they walked him free of the rocks, he started to remember again.

'Hurry!' he said. 'We must find an Ice Cucumber! Then we can defeat the dragon Borax!'

'Been there, done that, got the t-shirt!' explained Louis.

He did have the t-shirt too.

Look!

CHAPTER BANQUET

And finally, finally, finally . . . let's go back to the castle for a massive banquet. Why? Because it's the best way to end any story.

TUCK IN!

ACKNOWLEDGEMENTS

Thank you to the Knights of the Slightly Oblong Table: Sir Gaia Banks, Sir Bella Pearson, Sir Lucy Fawcett, Sir Amy Dobson, Sir Catherine Alport, Sir Colyn Allsopp, Sir Hannah Featherstone.

Thank you to our families for putting up with two hairy, bespectacled monsters. And especially to the real Louis for being the original audience of one.

Greg and Myles McLeod are known as The Brothers McLeod for two reasons. The first reason is that they have the same surname. The second reason is that they are brothers. They come up with silly stories together, then Greg draws the pictures and Myles writes the words. They have won things like a BAFTA and make cartoons for people like Disney, the Royal Shakespeare Company and Milkshake!

Have you read the first story about Knight Sir Louis?

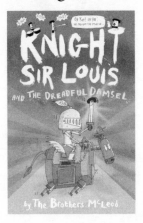

'Sublime daftness on every page!' Jeremy Strong

Knight Sir Louis is the champion knight at Castle Sideways, and the bravest of all knights in all lands. Braver than Knight Sir Colin in the bogs of Wattasmel. Braver than Knight Sir Barbara in the mountains of Itso-Hy. Even braver than Knight Sir Gary from the soggy lands of Tippinitdown.

But Louis is modest. He says he's not brave, but just good at staying calm when everyone else is going completely bonkers.

Along with his trusty mechanical steed, Clunkalot, and mystical sword, Dave, Knight Sir Louis and his friends are sent to do battle with the Damsel of Distresse who is terrorising the land, stealing coins of gold, silver and chocolate. But soon he finds himself dealing with strong enchantments, powerful magic, and evil potatoes . . . all in a normal day for this brave knight. (Just don't mention wasps.)

Hooray for Knight Sir Louis!

'A masterclass in silliness!' Gary Northfield

GUPPY BOOKS

Guppy Books is an independent children's publisher based in Oxford in the UK, publishing exceptional fiction for children of all ages.

Small and responsive, inclusive and communicative, Guppy Books was set up in 2019 and publishes only the very best authors and illustrators from around the world.

From funny illustrated tales for five-year-olds and magical middle-grade stories, to inspiring and thought-provoking novels for young adults, Guppy Books promises to publish something for everyone. If you'd like to know more about our authors and books, go to the Guppy Aquarium on YouTube where you'll find interviews, draw-alongs and all sorts of fun.

Bella Pearson
Publisher

www.guppybooks.co.uk